Love is
a time of enchantment:
in it all days are fair and all fields
green. Youth is blest by it,
old age made benign:
the eyes of love see
roses blooming in December,
and sunshine through rain. Verily
is the time of true-love
a time of enchantment — and
Oh! how eager is woman
to be bewitched!

THE FAIREST ONE OF ALL

Why was the most beautiful woman in Europe, and one of the richest, forced to live a vagabond's life? This is the story of Hortense Mancini, Duchess of Mazarin, one of the nieces of the famous Cardinal and heir to his wealth. Persecuted by her mad husband, she travelled from country to country in search of peace. Kings, princes and dukes were enslaved by her, but she preferred to have a child by an Italian coachman. Her reckless habits left her in poverty in London, where the one man who really loved her stayed with her until she died.

Books by Pamela Hill
Published by The House of Ulverscroft:

DIGBY
VOLLANDS
TREVITHICK
ANGELL & SONS
SUMMER CYPRESS
CURTMANTLE

PAMELA HILL

THE FAIREST ONE OF ALL

Complete and Unabridged

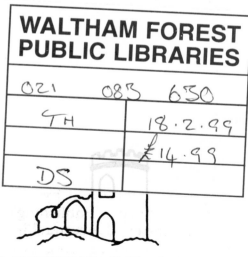
ULVERSCROFT
Leicester

First published in Great Britain in 1982 by
Robert Hale Limited
London

First Large Print Edition
published 1998
by arrangement with
Robert Hale Limited
London

British Library CIP Data

Hill, Pamela, *1920 –*
   The fairest one of all.—Large print ed.—
Ulverscroft large print series: romance
1. Love stories
2. Large type books
I. Title II. The fairest one of all
823.9'14 [F]

ISBN 0–7089–3978–3

Published by
F. A. Thorpe (Publishing) Ltd.
Anstey, Leicestershire
Set by Words & Graphics Ltd.
Anstey, Leicestershire
Printed and bound in Great Britain by
T. J. International Ltd., Padstow, Cornwall

This book is printed on acid-free paper

Mirror, mirror on the wall,
Who is the fairest one of all?

Old rhyme.

1

'These are not very grand apartments. It was better in Rome.'

'Be quiet, my child, you will be heard through the wall. Everyone at the Louvre hears everything, and then it runs through the palace on gossips' tongues and ends up quite differently from the way it began. Keep a still tongue in your head, and when you must speak at all, speak quietly.'

Hortense was not noticeably crushed; she was Mamma's favourite and knew it, unlike poor Marie who was crying in a corner because she had had her ears boxed again, nobody remembered why. As for the rest, Laura, whom they seldom saw since her marriage to M. de Mercoeur, sat quietly, like the visitor she was, and Olympe was looking at herself in the mirror and liking what she saw. Through it all Madame Hieronyma Mancini continued to talk, as though to improve on every occasion; after all a poor widow had to assert herself or else be forgotten by the world. Fortunately her brother was the Cardinal whom everyone obeyed. Like him Hieronyma was thin, with an acid personality; one wondered how she had contrived to produce so many beautiful daughters (there was still another, Marianne, left at her convent school) like dark fairies, all of them, except that Olympe's shoulders were too heavy.

'Royal palaces are seldom comfortable,' pronounced the widow. 'Even the Queen's apartments here are draughty, and she does her best with heavy hangings that blot out the light. But the honour of being invited to reside here is so great that it should not matter with it, naturally; seven years ago my sister and I — you were an infant in arms then, my Hortense, and Mamma had to leave you behind — I and your aunt Martinozzi came, and were received kindly by the Queen, who remarked on Olympe's beauty even then, and the two Lauras, your sister and your cousin, made good marriages.' Madame's mouth snapped shut; she could not forget that Laura Martinozzi had made much the more brilliant match of the two, to the Duke of Modena, and was never seen nowadays.

Marie, smarting in her corner, raised red-rimmed eyes towards Hortense, who winked, her long lashes lying on her cheek on the side Mamma could not see. Mamma had as usual forgotten to mention Philippe, who had been placed as a pupil with the Jesuits. Hortense missed Philippe more than anybody; when they were together they would write verse about one another.

Olympe, troubling for once with her family, turned her elegant head. 'When you meet the Queen, you will notice her beautiful perfumed arms and hands, although she is growing stout. When she was young she was so beautiful that the Duke of Buckingham was mad for her.'

'Be silent,' said Madame in horror. '*That* must never be mentioned here.'

'Why, Mamma?' enquired Hortense.

'Because I say so. Now, all of you, attend to your appearance and be as tidy as you can; we must pay our respects to your uncle.' Madame Hieronyma knew that this was the major hurdle, far more important than seeing the Queen. Giulio — she still thought of him as that — had stated firmly that he did not want a horde of indigent relatives descending on him again in Paris in search of noble husbands. But she could plead innocence of that; even Olympe was only thirteen, and as for Marie and Hortense, they had first been put to lodge in a convent from which she had only just taken them out. It did no harm to be seen.

Hortense also was thinking of the nuns,

and how pleasant it was to be free of their supervision, although Mamma's was almost as bad. She let her loose hair swing on her shoulders, glad of its silky feel. It was blue-black, the colour of a starling's wing, and curled naturally; she would never have to torture it with curl-papers like Marie and Olympe. She began to stray about the chamber, moving so lightly that the others, busied with their own affairs and talk, neither saw nor heard her. Presently she found a little door in the wall and opened it. It led to a small flight of steps and then to a passage. How full of passages the Louvre was! It did not matter if she got lost among them; someone would be sent to find her.

Excitement, which rose in her easily at any new thing, overcame her and she ran down the passage, anxious not to be found. At the end was a window such as could be seen anywhere on these upper floors of the palace, gabled outside and grey in colour, with the glass just above one's reach so that one must stand on tip-toe to see out. She did so, and looked down on Paris far beneath, spoiled by a drizzle of rain; the fruit and fish sellers had covered up their wares, and there were hardly any customers to be seen. Hortense wished Marie were here. Should she return for her? But Mamma might notice their both going, and that would mean more trouble for Marie; whatever the poor girl did was wrong. 'It is because she is not pretty as we are, and it will be more difficult to find her a husband,' thought the child practically. Yet Marie was clever and one need never be dull in her company. Of them all, one loved Marie best.

'What are you doing here, little girl? Have you lost your way, or are you listening at doors like everybody else?' The lazy voice was high and piping, like a girl's, but when Hortense spun round it was a boy who regarded her, not very tall, with dark curling hair and eyes and a full mouth like a woman's. She did not know who he was, but answered him back at once.

'I do not listen at doors. There is no need.'

He laughed, displaying pretty white teeth, and came closer; she could smell that he was scented. 'So you listen to gossip wherever you are?' he remarked. 'So do I; it can be useful. How pretty you are! I do not think I have ever seen such a lovely little creature. What is your name, my beauty?'

'Hortense Mancini. What is yours?'

'You may call me Philippe. We are going to be friends. Come and play hide and seek

5

with me. I am supposed to be with my tutor, but it does not signify. I will show you places to hide. Come.'

She let her small hand be taken in his soft white one. There was something odd about him, she had decided, but had not troubled to ask herself what it might be. He was as unlike her own brother Philippe as anyone could be. Her own Philippe would not trouble to play hide-and-seek with anyone. She hid, as it was her turn first, in a cupboard near a further flight of stairs; but this Philippe easily found her.

'I am allowed to kiss you for that,' he said, and she felt the full lips against her own. He enjoyed touching her; the soft white hands stroked her arms, her neck, her cheeks, her hair. 'How pretty you are!' he kept saying. 'How pretty you are, Hortense!'

'It is your turn to hide now,' she said. She did not want to hurt anyone who seemed friendly, but she was tired of being petted and caressed. He went off to hide, and when she had finished counting she opened doors, chests, cupboards, closets, looked behind hangings which were the worse for dirt and damp; but could not find him. There were people going to and fro, mostly women up here, in their rustling Court dresses with the new fashion of a wide band of lace about the

6

shoulders that some said the Queen had in fact brought long ago from Spain; but once a man spoke to her.

'Have you seen the Duc d'Anjou?' he queried, his eyes weary and his tones cold. Hortense shook her head, gazing up at him with great dark eyes. He smiled suddenly; she made everyone smile.

'He is a young boy aged thirteen,' he said. 'He is the King's brother. He should be at his lessons, and has played truant. He lives generally at the Palais-Royal, but it is being cleaned. If I do not find him the Queen must hear of it. If you should see him, tell him to come to me.'

She smiled, and promised; it was still intriguing to think that Philippe was the name of her own brother also. She had not yet met the King. Everyone said he was very handsome and a fine horseman and swordsman. He must be a great deal taller than this Anjou, who was hardly taller than herself. Who would have imagined him to be thirteen, the same age as Marie?

As soon as the tutor had gone Philippe himself slipped out of his hiding-place, and came to her. 'You did not say you had seen me,' he praised her. 'I love you, little Hortense. Shall we play again here tomorrow?'

'Hortense, where have you been? The Queen is to receive us at noon, and you must be laced into your best gown. How did you get so dusty? There is dirt on your face.' Laura Mercoeur, who had been sent to find her sister, stared accusingly; she herself was a tidy, unremarkable person who was seldom noticed or did anything out of place.

'It is a cobweb,' murmured Hortense, knowing Laura would not listen anyway; she had blundered into one in a cupboard when she had been playing with Philippe. She liked Philippe. She hoped it was true that he would come up here again, tomorrow at the same time, just to play with a little girl. Boys — her brother Paul was another — were as a rule superior beings, interested in other things such as swordplay. She herself would like to learn to use a sword, and to shoot, and —

Mamma shook her, scolded her briefly, then started to unlace her dress with the help of the Italian maid. All the rest were clad in their finery by now, and looked very well; Olympe in cherry satin, Laura in grey, poor Marie in *feuille morte* which did not become her sallow complexion, little Marianne in blue. 'You are to wear the ivory gown with yellow ribbons,' said Mamma, and Hortense permitted herself to be dressed like a doll, while the maid rubbed her face till it was clean; she must not, Mamma warned, let her feet show, for her shoes were shabby; they had not been able to buy everything. 'No doubt when your uncle finds time to receive us, it will be different.' Madame Hieronyma had a grimly determined reliance on the Cardinal, who so far had given no sign that he was any better pleased to see his sister and his nieces than he had been that time seven years ago. Well, one must be patient. Madame Mancini marshalled her brood and, with Marianne by the hand and Olympe keeping an eye on the rest, lest any again stray or get lost, she threaded her way down the interminable stairs and along the uneven passages. The Louvre was very old, creaking and damp. Many a noble lived in a better house than his King.

But the throne-room had grandeur. It was thronged with people, some of whom Hortense had already passed on her foray upstairs; they stared at her and whispered together, and she was pleased, for she knew they were commenting on her beauty; people always did. Somehow the party thrust its way through the wall of lace-banded shoulders and padded skirts to the throne, where a stout lady sat, clad in black; her skin was fair, her eyes heavy-lidded, and her rouged underlip jutted somewhat. This was Anne of Austria, Queen Regent of France; by her lounged a bored boy of about fifteen, clad in high soft riding-boots, for he was just going out; and a great plumed hat which sat becomingly on his abundant, rich dark curls. One would have known that he was the King from the fact that he had not, alone among so many, removed the hat; but somehow one knew also from the cool, knowing glance of the red-brown eyes, which were set obliquely, giving Louis Dieudonné, fourteenth of the name, the appearance of a young satyr. His features were beautifully modelled and his mouth proud. He has a good opinion of himself, thought Hortense.

On the other side of the Queen, occupying a small folding stool, sat her chief adviser and minister, Cardinal Mazarin, Madame Hieronyma's brother, thin and already pallid with the cancer which was to kill him. He saluted his sister and made known the young girls to the Queen, one after the other by name; but before it came to Hortense's turn a small figure had hurled itself down from the dais and piped in its high voice, 'This is Hortense, my playmate, Mamma. She is pretty, do you not think? We met upstairs.'

The company smiled at the impulsive abandon of the Duc d'Anjou, the King's younger brother; even Louis allowed his sculptured lips to turn up at the corners; but although Anne of Austria's full mouth smiled, her eyes were cold. She valued Jules Mazarin, whom some said she had married secretly; but she was not, and he knew it, prepared to raise all his impecunious relatives to positions of importance about Court. One would not, however, make a scene meantime. 'Indeed, Anjou?' she murmured in a low voice. 'Hortense is indeed pretty, if a trifle young for you.' She bent to where the child stood and spoke to her, naturally and kindly; Hortense made her curtsy, creditably, though her knees wobbled a trifle under her skirts. Already, she was thinking, I have made a friend of the King's brother; and the Queen has noticed me. Mamma should be pleased.

Suddenly she heard a voice droning behind her. 'In a few years those little girls will be worth castles, jewels, estates, fortunes. Note them, my friend.'

She felt the hot blood rise to her cheeks and longed to turn round, but that would be impolite. Whoever among the satin-coated, bewigged throng had said such a thing, she would never know. There was another thing she heard about herself. A Mazarinette. What was that? She would ask Olympe. It was pointless to ask Mamma, who would fly into a temper.

But Olympe had other business at the moment, for the King had noticed her. In fact she looked older than she was; her magnificent dark hair was dressed in a fashion suitable to a woman of twenty-five, and her young breasts showed round and full beneath the cherry-coloured satin. Louis guessed that she was too young, however, to pursue the acquaintance yet. His mind was already receptive to pretty women, ever since the day — how angry his mother had been! — one of her ladies-in-waiting had seduced him on his way back from his bath. That had been pleasant, and he deserved pleasure, for he worked hard every day; there was much serious business, to be discussed with the Cardinal, surveying state papers, making decisions — Mazarin he knew already permitted him a certain sufficiency of power — and that having been done, there was this stuffy crowd among which stood the promising young girl. When everything had abated and the introductions ceased, he would go out and exercise his hard young body in the saddle, riding far beyond the city which he loathed.

If only he could live in a palace surrounded by trees and water, far from smells and filth which greeted one in the Paris streets with their pestilent crowds! Later, later perhaps . . . everything he wanted would come later, including, if she were still available by then, the girl called Olympe.

Olympe was not the only one to be noticed. A young man standing among the crowd in the salon had fixed his eyes on Hortense. His expression remained rapt, as though he saw a goddess. His name was Armand de Porte de la Meilleraye, and he knew that the little girl at whom he was looking could be no more than ten years old. Nevertheless at that moment he swore he would make her his wife.

★ ★ ★

The days passed, and Hortense was to remember among them the awesome visit to her uncle, who received her and her mother and sister lying in a long chair; his rooms were full of servants in foreign clothes, precious cabinets, statues and portraits. Madame Hieronyma was ushered to a velvet-hung chair and exchanged the usual courtesies with her brother, whom she so seldom met; news of Rome and mutual friends

13

there both in and out of the Church; news of the Martinozzi cousins who had come on the previous visit, but not this. 'I hear Laura Martinozzi is at home with her grand marriage,' said His Eminence, his spiky dark eyebrows shooting up from his thin pasty face till they almost reached his biretta. Madame nodded, eagerly enough but as if she would like to put a finger to her lips.

'The Duke — nothing is said without discretion — our sister is overjoyed, her Laura has made a good and capable wife. I only wish mine were as biddable and well-mannered.'

'They all have beauty,' he murmured, and let a lock of Hortense's blue-black hair slide across his palm and between his fingers. He had already decided that she was the most taking of his nieces; Olympe was too blatant, Marie too plain, the rest not notable, not more than pretty. But Hortense would be a fiery beauty, with her flower-like skin and great eyes and silken hair. A marriage must be arranged for her that would not disgrace either her loveliness, or the fortune that he intended to leave her; yes, he had already decided it. He had heard — it was amusing in its way — that the little Duc d'Anjou had already developed a passion for Hortense, and would hardly let her out of his sight.

That, of course, could not be permitted to develop; Mazarin had no illusions about royal alliance; it was a pawn to be used in a game that involved all Europe. Soon, before she became dangerous, Hortense must be sent away, for a time; then brought back to Court, to a list of waiting suitors who could be considered on their merit, their title and fortune. His thin lips smiled as his eyes regarded the child. He said to her, 'You play chess, my dear, I believe?'

'Yes, yes, Philippe has taught me, that and battledore, and hide and seek, and — '

Madame Hieronyma had opened her pursed lips to silence her daughter; children should not chatter, only answer clearly when they were addressed; that was one of the things Hortense would have to learn. But the Cardinal raised a finger, smiling, and she remained silent.

'Who wins the games of chess, my child? You, or the Duc d'Anjou?' He stressed Philippe's title; the use of the familiar name must be discouraged.

'I won once, when he let me. But generally he wins. He says he would like to be a general, disposing soldiers. That is why he is so good at chess. It is like an army, only much slower.'

The Cardinal winced; a spasm of pain

had shot through him. He closed his eyes briefly and then opened them again. 'Go to Mustapha, with Marianne, and he will give you Turkish sweetmeats,' he said gently. The children ran off, and he turned his attention to his sister. Her dark eyes were unfathomable. 'You are not a fool, Nounou,' he said, addressing her by the name he had used to call her when they were children together, in their Sicilian village. 'You know, I think, that we must send the little one away.'

'Send Hortense from me? But she is dearer to me than any of them. If it had been that dreary Marie, how glad I should have been! How I am to find her a husband I do not know, she is so plain, and does nothing to better herself, forever with her nose in a book. But take away Hortense? Why, Giulio?'

'Because the younger brother of the King of France must not be permitted to grow up as a man who likes pretty girls and the command of soldiers. Too much trouble was caused in such ways in the late reign. Hortense must go, but only meantime; in a year or two, when we have moulded Anjou more suitably for our purpose, it will be safe for her to return.'

'But where am I to send her? The last

convent was expensive, and I have all the rest to bring forward.'

His smile widened. 'You were never slow to ask, Nounou, were you? Of course I shall pay. I should like to remind you also — you are bound to have heard it already — of what the Court, and even the ballad-singers in the streets, had to say on the last occasion you and our sister and her brood, and yours, visited me last time in Paris. They spoke of the Mazarinettes — '

'What impudence!'

'But apt. I called in the broadsheets. This time again they are saying that, owing to my acquisitive habits, every one of these little girls will bring castles, titles, jewels, to a husband. Take comfort, my Nounou; your Hortense will not waste her years in the convent.'

★ ★ ★

Hortense and Anjou sat down to their last game of chess. It was not she, but the boy himself, who had been crying; his long lashes still showed traces of tears.

'Will you take the red?' said Hortense. 'Do not cry, Philippe.'

'It does not matter.' He pushed a pawn out of place. 'I am like one these; to be made

17

use of as they choose. You know, do you not, that they are sending you away because I love you so?'

'Not that. They told me nothing, simply that I am to go back to school.'

'So that I may not see you, and will forget you,' said Anjou bitterly. 'When I had model soldiers they took them away also, lest I become a better commander than my brother. The King must excel in all he does. I, the younger, they will turn into . . . an abomination. I know it, though I cannot explain. I cannot talk to others as I can to you.'

Hortense did not know what an abomination was, but saw that he was sad. She leaned over and kissed him. 'When I come back, you may still talk to me all you like,' she said. 'I shall not change.'

'I wish that I need not.' He reached out and took her knight, and Hortense clapped her hands generously.

'There,' she said. 'You are still a good commander of soldiers.'

2

It was galling to have been sent back to school at the convent as though in disgrace, when all that she had done had been to be pretty enough to attract the King's brother. She missed her sisters, also, especially Marie: Marianne, who had been left with her, was too young to be good company. It was not possible to write freely because letters were supervised; so Hortense spent a great deal of time pretending to read, idly setting out card games, gossiping with the other young ladies among whom she soon made a special friend, and dreaming of Court, which she had seen so briefly. What were they all doing at this moment, when she herself sat by a latticed window looking out at the rain, or inwards at the inevitable silent grace of the sisters' robes as they went about their duties? It would be impossible to be a nun. If only the time would pass, and the day come when Mamma and the Cardinal had promised she might return! What would have happened to poor Anjou by then? It did not matter; she had almost forgotten his face, though she remembered the caressing white hands.

They will turn me into an abomination. Was it happening? Could anyone stop it? My uncle the Cardinal could, she thought inconsequentially. She thought of Mazarin's smooth, strong will, which achieved all he wished; a man who governed France would not think it important to alter the lives of a boy and a girl. What did he intend for herself? Marriage, no doubt. She found that she had no clear picture of the man she would like to marry, which was just as well. One accepted what came, that was all.

She knew that she did not love the Cardinal, though he was fond of her. She had done his will, spoken courteously to him, nowadays wrote him dutiful letters from time to time, and that was all. What would happen when he died? Everyone said he had not long to live, but they had been saying that for years. It was as though the iron will kept the frail body alive. Hortense stretched out her own white firm arm and studied its texture. It was as beautiful as Queen Anne's, with rose-tipped fingers, though too thin because she was still a child. If only the time would pass!

'Attend to your duties, Hortense,' said the passing sister gently. To nuns, idleness was of Satan; they always occupied themselves, when they were not praying, with this task or that. Hortense picked up the sewing she was supposed to be at and made tiny pricks in the linen with the needle. One stroked it and then stitched it, and then there was a neat garment to wear. She did not care about stitchery. The time would come when she would choose chemises made delicately by others, embellished with rare lace and embroidery; and the gowns she would have would be all colours, made of Genoa velvet, figured, looped in gold, and satin brocade, and sleeves sewn with pearls, and more pearls in her hair. That was how she would appear before them next time at Court; well, perhaps not quite next time, but when she married. There was nothing to wait for, after all, but that.

* * *

One thing however happened to her in the two years she spent at the convent out of Philippe d'Anjou's way; it became the fashion among the younger girls to follow and serve her, pick up her handkerchief when she had dropped it, share their marchpane and raisins with her, admire her dresses and ribbons, try to copy the way she did her hair. All her life Hortense would be the object of such devotion, and hardly noticed it. Women

21

loved her as Diana had been loved by her nymphs.

★ ★ ★

The time came when the Cardinal decreed that Hortense might return to Court, and soon she saw what had happened to poor Philippe; he no longer cared for her, and instead was besotted by a young man named de Choisy, in whose company he would dress up as a girl, combing his long dark curls into locks beneath a wide hat, walking mincingly in his long petticoats and high red heels. Hortense thought it a jest and decided that, for her part, she would not at all mind dressing as a boy; breeches were more convenient, and one could stride about with a sword by one's side, and fight duels. But Mamma, of course, would never permit such a thing. Mamma permitted very little these days. She had grown old, and thinner than ever; there was much grey in her hair and she did not trouble to dye it. She still took time to parade Olympe in fine clothes, because the King had taken a fancy to her and partnered her frequently in the dance, so that she might well attract a high-born husband. 'As for me,' muttered Marie, 'she never lets me go to a ball; she locks me up here by the hour.

Fortunately one can read.'

Hortense was horrified, hearing the lilting music in her mind to which Marie would never dance, Olympe always. 'That is unfair,' she said hotly. 'We will tell my uncle. He can make Mamma do anything.'

Marie's lips tightened a little over the book she had been holding. She had altered little in two years; she was still thin, brown of complexion, undistinguished except for the magnificent eyes. Suddenly she burst out crying. 'We dare not do that,' she sobbed. 'It would be the worst thing for all. Mamma has told the Cardinal that I have an evil nature and should be forced to take the veil. I dare not bring myself to his attention. He has never loved me, any more than Mamma has ever done.'

'*I* love you,' said Hortense, and it was true; rather than Olympe with her grandeur and sullens, or the respectably married Laura, or witty little Marianne, she loved Marie best; Marie who was plain but clever, in whose company one was never dull, who must be helped, and quickly, somehow, anyhow. Marie had already given her a little caress for saying she loved her; now she wiped away her tears and said, 'Forgive me for being stupid. It is because I am left so much alone.'

'Do you still paint, Marie?'

'Why, what — '

Hortense rose from her place and twirled her skirts with joy. 'We will make a plan,' she said. 'You know, and Mamma knows, that our uncle is fond of me even though I do not greatly like him. You must paint a portrait of me to send to him, and then he will be pleased with us both. We must use him against Mamma. I am certain that we can do it, if we are careful.'

She had set herself against the most dexterous statesman in France, but it did not deter her; even the return of Mamma and Olympe, full of gossip about the next coming ball, only half reached her, so busy was she planning the dress she would wear to be painted by Marie.

* * *

Madame Mancini had been in indifferent health, and it so happened that on a certain day she went out driving in the carriage with Olympe, to take to the air. It so happened, also, that the King, as he frequently did, called at the house Madame had taken to be free of the cramped quarters they had vacated at the Louvre. His excuse was to enquire for Madame's health, his reason to see Olympe. The latter's quickly-maturing bloom, which she would soon lose, was appreciated by him as a young male; he had no interest in her lack of conversation or concern with her bad temper, which in any case she never manifested while he was present. Recently Olympe had had a swollen head in any case, because lately at a ball Louis had danced with her a dance which should by rights have belonged to the Princess of England, who was only a child. 'My daughter has hurt her foot,' interposed the widowed Queen of England hastily. 'I do not like little girls,' murmured Louis to Olympe as they turned away together in the great panache of the *promenade à deux*. Olympe's black curls shook and her dimples came and went; her breasts had developed by now to a degree which could excite a man.

So Louis had come today. As fortune had it, the maid who would in the ordinary way have answered the door was sick in bed, and an inferior who knew nothing, and had just arrived, took her place. When the tall and handsome young man enquired tenderly for Madame Mancini, she replied, 'Madame has driven out, so please you. But the young ladies are at home, upstairs.'

'Then I will announce myself to the young ladies,' replied Louis, and strode across the hall towards the staircase. He did not need to be shown which room to enter, as he had been in it before; a kind of parlour, where Madame received her guests with her daughters in an arranged circlet about her, like a wreath of flowers.

But today there were only two, and Olympe was not there. There was the minx Hortense, whom everybody knew, and who was having her portrait painted by a thin girl in a long overall of unbleached linen, palette and brushes in her brown hands. Perhaps Louis noticed the hands first; they were not plump, like Olympe's, but showed the slender bones. The painting stopped as the model jumped down and said, 'Oh, good, Marie! Here is the King. Now we shall not be dull.'

Louis bowed, amused, his carefully dressed curls falling forward to hide his face. When he straightened again, the painter was still where she had been, as though stricken by immobility into a statue. Her eyes had widened; they were fine eyes, like great liquid pools. 'Why do I never see you at Court?' enquired the King, who was not accustomed to restrain his desire for information. Hortense came pushing in, fluffing out her skirts which had grown crushed with posing. 'It is because Mamma will never allow Marie to attend balls, and locks her up here and is trying to make her become a nun.'

'Hortense, you should not — ' began the thin girl, then smiled despite herself, laid aside her palette and paints, and made her curtsy now that her hands were free. 'Do not listen to the child,' she begged the King. 'She prattles too much.'

'But is it true of what she prattles, that you are not permitted to attend Court balls? I myself have never seen you at one, and had I done so I should not have forgotten, mademoiselle.'

His eyes had never left her face, and under their steady scrutiny she coloured, becoming, for that instant, beautiful. 'It is true,' she said, and turned her head away. 'But I do not mind greatly; I am happier reading a book.'

'What books do you read, Mademoiselle Marie?' He himself had let that part of his education become neglected, so eager had he been to prove himself that his body was strong, lithe, the perfect servant to his will. Now, he regretted it.

She had lifted her narrow shoulders in the tiniest shrug. 'Sire, I read what I may; whatever is to hand. I read Racine a great

27

deal. I admire his poetry.'

'Come, recite some Racine for me.'

'I cannot — I am not accustomed to — I — '

'Do not heed her,' said Hortense. 'She would do credit to the stage itself. She can imitate anyone, even an old woman or an invalid, to make us all laugh. She — '

'You talk too much, Mademoiselle Hortense. It would be better did your sister talk more and you less. Come, as you have so many words: command her for me.' He smiled; insinuatingly, as though Hortense herself were already a grown woman. In fact sensations he had never before experienced were amazing him; he was both glad and sorry for the younger sister's presence. She was as the painted canvas represented her; pert, pretty, good-natured, spoilt, and unthinking as a sunbeam.

'You are commanded, mademoiselle,' he told Marie. 'Do you disobey your King?'

Ah, but he such a boy, she thought, prey to like sensations. Olympe would not have satisfied him for long. Fear that Mamma and Olympe might return from the drive consumed her, and she began, without lowering her eyes, to recite gently, almost mournfully,

It is not mine to assure an easy triumph,
Nor place a tranquil sceptre in your
  hands;
But all that I can do, as I have promised,
I arm your valour 'gainst your enemies,
And from your head remove a threatening
  danger.
Your own firm courage will achieve the
  rest.

It was finished. For an instant Louis, King of France, sat immobile, the greatest compliment he had ever paid to a woman. Then he rose from where he had been sitting, took both her hands, and kissed them, paint-daubed as they were, first on the backs, then on the palms.

'You shall appear at the next Court ball,' he said. 'You are again commanded. I can see that I am going to have to command many things from you, Mademoiselle Marie.'

3

'The King is in love with Marie Mancini!'

The talk spread, echoed, rebounded on itself, was denied, then, once more, agreed upon. His Majesty walked, talked, listened to, watched, danced with, the most unattractive of the Mazarinettes, the one who had always been hidden away. Those who overheard their talk soon grew bored; it concerned poetry. Undoubtedly the King was bewitched. Of what the Cardinal had to say, little was known; of what Marie's mother said, speculation was lacking. Even she, who detested her daughter, might well be proud to see her married to the King of France.

The King was at war. He besieged a place named Malmédy, near Liége. Afterwards — it was a victory — Louis fell ill of a fever, and in his ramblings called for Marie; no one else would do. She was sent for, and sat by him, applying cool cloths to his fevered forehead, holding her hand in his as if to reassure him. 'Marie, Marie,' he would call.

'I am here, my dear Sire. I will not leave you.'

But others thought differently. When the King was convalescent he walked with Marie, holding her hand, by the river at Bois-le-Vicomte near Fontainebleau. As they walked his heavy sword-hilt chafed her wrist raw, and she bit her lip but made no complaint. When the evening came to an end the King turned her hand upwards to kiss it, and saw the wounding. 'What has done this?' he said angrily. She smiled.

'Your sword, Sire. It is an honourable wound.'

He wrenched his sword from the scabbard, and flung it into the river. It might have been a gesture in one of the plays they loved to discuss. Other gestures were made by him to her, whom he now called, in public, his queen. One day he threaded a rare necklace of pearls about her throat; they had been bought by Charles the First of England for his bride, Henrietta Maria, who had since had to sell them to live. The widowed Queen of England could not hide her tears when she saw them encircling Marie's brown throat.

She was too proud to speak of it to any, but the Cardinal had already heard; he sat in his heated rooms one evening, and surveyed a map of Spain. That strange country had once ruled half the world, still owned half of it, but was engulfed in mediaeval night and would never be great again. Yet he had the King of Spain's assurance that an alliance between his young master, Louis XIV, and the Infanta Maria Teresa would be welcome. Mazarin frowned, then tapped a certain signal on his table-top. At once there was a sound of oiled hinges sliding open, the rustle of skirts, and Anne of Austria was in the room.

'Do not rise,' she said, for she knew he was ill. 'You have news for me?' She surveyed him, this man whom popular accord said was her lover, her husband; they had said many things of her, and she had outlived them all. His thin yellow hand pointed to a place, Madrid, on the map; she knew it well enough; her youth had been spent there. 'Is there no word?' she murmured fearfully.

'Only that, if my niece stays about the King, His Majesty the King of Spain will reconsider the favourable reception he has given to the suggestion of marriage between our King here and the Infanta.'

'That must not be. It would mean war again, as there was in former times.' She raised her beautiful white hand to her plump breast, and felt its throbbing; Louis must, he must, be induced to agree to this Spanish offer! Anything else left France powerless in the midst of her foes, the Rhineland, England, the rest.

'I have sent for him tonight. If you will stay here, we may persuade him together. Otherwise he is stubborn, as you know.'

'Tonight?' Fear took her; she always avoided direct scenes, direct approaches. It would be as it had once been when her lover, the madman Buckingham, had trapped her in a garden to try to make love, but she had cried out and her ladies had come. There had been no slur on her reputation, but she had longed for Buckingham ever since. He had been murdered by a fanatic on his return to England. Still, night after night, Anne prayed for his soul. Love . . . who could describe it? And now Louis thought himself in love. It happened to young people; their wounds would heal.

The door was flung open and her son stood there, erect and unafraid. 'You sent for me?' he said to the Cardinal, making a brief deference to his mother. He will soon be King indeed, she thought; he will take telling from no one. Affection for him flooded her, as though it were fear.

The Cardinal spoke. 'It is gracious of Your Majesty to spare an old man an hour,' he said. 'It will not be more, I promise you.'

'What would you with me?' The King spoke impatiently; Marie was waiting for him, by arrangement, and the two of them were to read *Polyeucte* together, each one acting different parts. The widening of his mind had unleashed a new sense of power in him. If he could marry Marie, wise learned Marie, together they could create a new kingdom, a new world. Yet confronted not only with the man who all his youth had wielded power in France, and also with his mother whom he revered, Louis was cautious; not afraid, for there was no fear in him; but he must handle this matter carefully.

'Be seated, my son; there are only the three of us,' said Anne. According to the rule of etiquette neither she nor Mazarin should have remained seated in the presence of His Majesty; and Mazarin was ill.

'I will not, but do you both remain so,' said Louis curtly. He had a shrewd notion there was something they wanted of him; he would be on his guard. He was right; Mazarin spoke.

'Your Majesty knows that there have been certain negotiations proceeding with the King of Spain regarding Your Majesty's marriage with the Infanta Doña Maria Teresa.'

'I neither want to marry Doña Maria Teresa nor any other woman in the world except — you know of it already — your niece, Marie Mancini. I desire her for my queen and none other. Do not deny me.'

'My son — a commoner . . . ' Anne of Austria had risen from her place, her cheeks white beneath their rouge. 'It cannot be! You can wed none such.'

'It is the desire of my heart — '

'If we all followed the desires of our hearts, what chaos would kingdoms be in! My son, it is your duty, as you know, to marry the Infanta of Spain.'

'My manhood denies my duty. I have a woman whom I love, whose mind is in tune with mine. Can the Infanta of Spain bring me the contentment I find with Marie? Answer me, you who are her uncle. Would it suit you so ill to see her Queen of France?'

Mazarin traced a pattern on the table with his finger. 'My son, it is your duty to marry the Infanta. She is neither beautiful nor intelligent, but should you not marry her, Europe will be at war.'

'Europe!' said Louis, half weeping. He suddenly knelt, holding out his strong hands to his mother and the Cardinal. 'Grant me this — let me marry Marie, and all power shall be yours. I can grant you honours you have not dreamed of. I can — '

'You are talking to a dying man, my son; and talking in a manner unworthy of a King of France.'

35

'Rise, Louis,' said his mother sharply. 'Do not kneel there like a servant. There is no one in the land or beyond to whom you should kneel, saving our Holy Father the Pope. You are the anointed of God, the direct son of Clovis. Do not behave like a young attorney whose girl has been taken away from him. What will the world think? How it will laugh!'

Her speech stung him, and he stumbled to his feet. 'But Marie? What of her?'

The Cardinal spoke smoothly. 'Marie will be married in due course to the only son of the Duc de la Meilleraye. Give her the chance to find her own happiness. You yourself can fall in love with many women, possess them, forsake them for others as you choose. You are the King of France, and no man's servant.'

★ ★ ★

In fact, the only son of the Duc de la Meilleraye, having observed Marie Mancini, had already decided that she was in any case too plain. Her sister Hortense, however young . . . 'If God will grant me but three months of life, I will marry her and none other!'

Hortense was still unaware of the hot gaze

of the loose-mouthed young man focussed upon her; some days later, she forgot him and everyone else in anger; despite her and Marie's plans to bring the Cardinal to their side, he had stated that Hortense was to be sent back to the convent again. 'It is my fault,' murmured Marie, fingering the pearls she always wore and would not part with were she starving. She had grown even thinner in these days, and more quiet. Mamma was very ill and thought to be dying. Poor Mamma, thought Hortense; no one cared.

She herself was bundled into a coach and returned to the convent just as Armand de Meilleraye, her undeclared suitor, King Philip III of Spain, the Cardinal, and King Louis were at loggerheads. Ready to burst into tears, Hortense watched the familiar roads flash past; time would be slow, in the convent. Why did her uncle the Cardinal pretend that she was his favourite, and yet do nothing for her but send her back here?

4

Long afterwards, Hortense would sometimes try to recall the rituals which had accompanied her own growing up, leaving her hardly time to notice the latter; the death of Mamma, the weddings, and the coming back to Court of Marianne. She found it impossible to arrange everything in the order in which it happened, so tended to think disagreeably, first, of tubby little Marianne, the youngest sister, who became the Cardinal's and Queen Mother's pet, and was taught by her uncle to listen at doors to report what Marie was saying and doing. Hortense caught her at it several times and slapped her furiously, but it was like hitting a shuttlecock; it simply sailed away, later to return. In any case it did not matter now about the King and Marie; the Peace of the Pyrenees was signed, the Spanish marriage was arranged, and Marie spent hours crying on her bed till no one would have thought there could be as many tears. They had made a tender farewell, she and Louis; that was all, and there was nothing more on which to spy. Yet her uncle would be assured of every least thing; Hortense had begun to dislike him very much. He could never move straight towards an obstacle, but always crabwise, seeking how best to attack it from the side or the rear; in such a way he had married Olympe to the Comte de Soissons, reasoning that by this cause she would be put out of the way of the King. Hortense remembered the creamy bridal lace on Olympe's dark hair, and her sullen expression as she took the marriage vows; she knew very well what it was all for. As for the Comte, nobody noticed him, except to remark that his name was ancient.

But Marie . . .

'I used to try to help them,' Hortense would remind herself, thinking of those who had come with the King. 'I used to sit and converse with them, or play cards or some ridiculous game, so that he and she could talk together alone.' But it had all been useless. Then into her mind would float the silliest game of all, in which the Cardinal would try to convince fat Marianne that she was pregnant. 'Loosen her stays! Do not confine her! It will be any moment now!' and the like, and even Anne of Austria had laughed and had offered to be the baby's godmother. One day they had hired a new-born baby and put it in

Marianne's bed so that she would find it when she awoke. 'I never felt a single pain,' she protested. 'This has only happened to Our Lady and to me. And it must be either the King's baby or the Comte de Guiche's, for nobody else has kissed me.'

It was all very amusing, and in the meantime the Cardinal had been hurrying on the bridals, for he knew he would not live long. Marie was to be married to the Prince Colonna, who lived in Rome and Naples and whom she had never seen. Hortense herself had had an offer of which she did not hear until many years afterwards; if only they had told her at the time! Charles II, the exiled King of England, was looking for a rich wife; and as it seemed likely that Hortense would inherit the bulk of the Cardinal's fortune he had offered for her, and had been courteously refused. If only ... but he had been suffered to move on, that very tall dark ugly stranger, whose love and hers could have been notable, whose children both brilliant and many. 'They told him, for excuse, that La Grande Mademoiselle must be married first,' she reflected. Poor Charles had also tried that bean-pole, without obtaining Mademoiselle's fortune either.

The King of Spain had actually withdrawn his approval of the alliance with the Infanta, because of Marie. The affair had been hastily patched up. Hearts did not matter. In the meantime all her brothers and male cousins had had something happen to them; Alphonse, the heir, whom none of them knew, had died; Paul had decided to enter a monastery; Philippe Martinozzi, the cousin, was an idle useless creature who only made trouble. The Cardinal loathed him. So it was she, Hortense, who would inherit. Of course she would share everything; would share with poor Marie, even with Olympe, perhaps with Marianne if she grew pleasanter. There would be a husband of one's own by then, but he did not matter.

The Cardinal, she knew, had meant to do better for her. He had considered her as Queen of Portugal, but that might have caused the enmity of Spain; even d'Anjou of old days — he was Duc d'Orléans now after the death of his uncle, and as frippery as ever — was thought of! The Duke of Savoy had fallen in love with her in Lyons, while the river flowed past; also the Prince de Courtenay, the greatest aristocrat in France, but with no money. Moreover he was a pervert. Savoy, therefore, was considered before everyone, but lost Hortense through his own greed; he wanted to be given back the fortress of Pignerol as part of the dowry, and Pignerol had been won within living memory, with much expense and blood, for France by the late King. So one had to start again.

* * *

The King travelled to a midway meeting-place that summer and was married to the Infanta, a portly little person loaded with emeralds for the occasion. His nature had changed; it was as though he had been through fire. When he thought of Marie nowadays it was with pity; her marriage must be hastened on, she must leave France soon, for her own sake. As for the rest, there were no more Pyrenees. He returned to Paris in a triumphal procession reminiscent of the ancient Romans, with himself the centre of it, riding beneath a white canopy, and the little Queen in a carriage behind. In such circumstances he could forget that her teeth were spoiled with chocolate, her breath with garlic, and she had no conversation. From this hour, he was King of France, with power unlimited; the Cardinal, who had made the marriage, would not live long.

* * *

Hortense and Marie had chosen finery for the wedding festivities, but Marie spoilt it by bursting into tears the moment her eyes caught sight of any dress of her own the King had ever seen. Since Mamma's death the house was like a cauldron, ready to spurt out burning matter at any moment; everyone flew into a passion for no reason, everyone did as she chose. The Cardinal, who took his charge of his nieces seriously, visited a duenna upon them. Her name was Madame Venel. She was as might have been expected; dull, prying, vulnerable to whatever devilment Hortense and Marianne could devise. At night the good lady, instructed by the Cardinal, stole through the bed-chambers passing her hand over her charges' beds; one night there was a prodigious yell. 'I bit her,' said Marianne smugly. Another time they gave her a box of sweetmeats which when opened, proved to be full of live mice. The mice escaped, Madame gasped and, to everyone's delight, swooned. Her life was a misery, but she was indispensable; someone or other had to supervise the stubbornly unmarried Mazarinettes.

At Court, everything had changed. The King's brother, beribboned Monsieur, Duc d'Orléans, who had once been ready to worship the child Hortense, was married to

Princess Henrietta of England now that her brother Charles II had regained his throne. Nobody expected the couple to be happy.

★ ★ ★

Madame de Venel had made her report. Olympe, petulant at Hortense's gibe (which was true) that she still fancied the King, had made one also. As a result, Hortense was called to the Cardinal's presence. When she was announced he rose, kissed her hand, and bade her be seated. Then he subjected her to a long scrutiny with those cold eyes which had raised fear in many a civil servant. But behind the cold gaze his mind was warm. How divinely lovely the child was! A child, no more; perhaps a child too long; good-natured to a degree, no doubt. It was difficult to scold her as he ought to do. If only she could regard him with affection! If only there did not have to be this distance between them, he a Prince of the Church and she . . . a rogue. Could they not love one another a little? Love had been so lacking in his life . . . he had loved the late King, Louis XIII. Perhaps in process of changing from Giulio Mazzarini to Jules Mazarin, copying in everything his master Richelieu, he himself

44

had hardened and altered. No doubt it came to everyone.

He watched Hortense swing her tiny satin slipper. The heedless act itself was almost an outrage, implying lack of respect for him, the great Cardinal and arbiter of her life. He thought of a thing to say. 'Why do you not attend Mass daily?' he asked her. 'Madame Venel tells me you seldom go.'

Hortense shrugged her white shoulders and he was suddenly exasperated. 'You have neither piety nor honour!' he shouted. He felt the sick blood rush to his head and grasped the table's edge. 'At least,' he heard a faraway voice, which was his own, saying, 'if you do not hear it for God's sake, hear it for the world's.'

Hortense still said nothing. Everyone heard Mass for the world's sake; they liked to flaunt their new *toilettes*. Also each morning after the King had spent the night with her — it happened once a month — the Queen took communion, which was diverting. But she herself had diversions of her own. 'Have you a particular admirer?' had chattered Madame Venel in her prying way. 'I am in love,' Hortense had replied solemnly, 'with an Italian musician.' The effect on the good lady had been almost as bad as the mice. Who was this musician? What was his name? How had they met? A goggle-eyed lutanist, thriving on the gossip, had appeared below Hortense's windows to serenade her ever since, until Madame chased him; she herself had no idea who he was and did not care. To be sought by many was like wine, heady and exciting; better than being like poor Marie, who was saying now that she would rather marry the Duke of Lorraine than the Colonna, but in fact cared nothing for either of them.

Hortense opened her eyes wide; her uncle had begun to speak of it. 'Two ladies desire the Duke of Lorraine,' he said smoothly, 'one your sister and one the younger daughter of the late Monsieur, who is already betrothed to the Duke of Tuscany. It is a coil indeed, and one cannot blame older heads for thinking of practical matters first and the heart afterwards. Who is your musician?'

'I do not know.'

'Are you stupid, as the Court is beginning to say, or merely lacking in interest? It is your future of which I speak, Hortense. You are at least not as bad as your sister Marianne, for whom I am having to engage a tutor; poor Madame de Venel is at her wits' end with her.'

I know, thought Hortense; and the abbé whom they are engaging for Marianne is called the Man of a Thousand Mistresses.

She giggled suddenly, causing the Cardinal's brows to draw together. 'Why do I trouble myself with any of you?' he said irritably. 'Why do I not leave my fortune to the nation I have protected? Your sister Olympe has caused scandal by telling the King Marie is Lorraine's mistress. Your brother Philippe has taken part in an escapade in a country-house wherein he edified everyone by killing a pig and with others in a like state, said Mass over it. Such escapades are not amusing to persons of taste.'

He rose, and dismissed her; nothing, after all, had been decided about her marriage. She cared little, as life at present was diverting and presented no responsibilities.

5

Cardinal Mazarin was holding one of his great receptions; as it turned out, the last of his life. As if he knew this, everything was gilded, scented, spiced as never before; the great paintings and statues he had amassed seemed to waver behind moving spirals of smoke from perfumed pastilles, burnt to keep away the dreaded stench of cancer. The Cardinal himself was scented also; his robe, his gloves, the furry pet monkey on a jewelled chain which sat on his shoulder. He liked to have small animals about him, just as in his day the great Richelieu had diverted himself playing with kittens. Mazarin received his guests graciously, for they were of the highest rank in France; the King, the Queen, the Queen Mother, little Monsieur and his new bride Henrietta of England, who on her marriage had changed overnight from the mouse-like creature she had formerly been to something so gay, so charming, so irresistible that it was whispered that the King himself did not, in fact, resist. Both brides were pregnant. Behind them followed the Court; the Comte and Comtesse de Soissons,

Olympe in a gown that stood out among the rest like a pasque-flower among rosebuds; all of Hortense's suitors, the penniless Savoy in a glittering coat, Armand de Meilleraye in nothing notable; no doubt he held so high an opinion of himself that what he wore was of no account. He brooded alone among the statuary, his eyes fixed burningly on Hortense, who was not aware of him, or not particularly so; in fact she found it diverting that a man had been in love with her since she was ten years old. Plump little Marianne had been permitted to attend, with Madame de Venel and the Man of a Thousand Mistresses in close attendance; and those who watched, those who wrote memoirs and would record every item of this night, were in the forefront, sharp eyes bright beneath curled perukes, keen minds avid for scandal. But there was no scandal in the Cardinal's house; after the musicians had played and the fruit-flavoured ices and other delicacies had been passed round, he announced a novelty; there was to be a raffle, and everyone would win a prize from the precious things carefully displayed on marquetry tables in an inner room. Sidling in front of the crowd, for she always liked to choose before anyone, was a young woman whose beauty was not yet at its full height; by contrast with Hortense, the loveliest woman present, this arrival looked pudding-faced and dull; yet her wit and her name were both well known; she was Madame de Montespan. She fastened her large blue eyes on a grotesque thing which sat among the objects to be won; a chair-lift, which conveyed the sick Cardinal from floor to floor. His yellowed eyes surveyed her, and he smiled a little.

'To have to leave all this!' he said, and she knew then that he knew he was dying. That meant that the marriage of that minx, Hortense, must be settled soon, for she was his heir. Athénaïs de Montespan waited for the next move; the crowd rustled in, pursuing their separate treasures. She herself had won a small ivory ape, and stared down at it squatting in her palm. Her husband, who was *farouche*, had not come tonight. She would give him the ape to mock him.

Anne of Austria stayed near her daughter-in-law, who still had made no friends. The two women resembled one another in the full Hapsburg lip and the white, plump flesh of the royal house of Spain; one of them had been beautiful, the other never would be. Marie-Thérèse had flaxen hair, Anne's was brown with a hint of grey, its former famed golden glints eclipsed. Age was settling slowly upon her in the form of white fat; she had yet no means of knowing, as she watched poor Jules Mazarin eaten by disease, that in a few years her own opulent flesh would wither and corrode under this same scourge with its stink of death; that her son and his wife would kneel side by side in her perfumed, darkened bedchamber to say farewell. Tonight was, however, not the time to think of such things; everyone must sparkle in wit as in jewels, smooth in response as the satins they wore; to smile, not weep, was fashionable. But though she kept her full lip curved agreeably Anne of Austria was sad. She would miss Jules Mazarin; she had come to rely on him for many things; and although the King had been trained by him and was a worthy product of that training, how strong Louis' will had grown! It had been like breaking a sword to force him to give up Marie Mancini, who in the nature of things must be sent out of France, and the sooner the better.

6

January held the country in its bitter grip: all France awaited the birth of a Dauphin. In the Mazarin palace, a cadaver waited for death; few saw him now, but one day there was announced a visitor of some importance. The Bishop of Fréjus was admitted, with weighty business. He sat by the bed of the dying Cardinal, having kissed his ring.

'My news will bring you joy, I hope.' His voice, accustomed to bring emotion to large congregations, had lessened its volume to fit the small room, the curtained bed. The stench was — ugh! He hastened his business, eager to be gone.

'It concerns,' he said, 'my young friend Armand de la Porte de Meilleraye, who these many years has desired Your Eminence's niece Hortense for his wife.'

The skeleton on the bed frowned. 'De Meilleraye's grandfather was a lawyer. He is not of the first rank.'

The Bishop permitted himself a smile. Was Giulio Mazzarini indeed speaking? 'There are few of us who do not have a lesser inheritance mingled with our admitted one,' he conceded. 'The King himself has Jewish and Moorish blood mixed with that of Henri IV and the House of Valois. I may say this to you, who are discreet. Note it, and reconsider the matter of these lovers; let them be man and wife.'

'Hortense has never loved anyone but herself . . . and Marie, a little. Poor Marie . . . '

The Bishop had not come to talk of Marie. 'Then you will admit the claim of young de Meilleraye? No suitor is more ardent than he, or has waited as long.' No suitor, he might have added, had offered him, the Bishop, fifty thousand crowns if he could bring about the consummation of the marriage. There were not, as far as one could see, a press of suitors for Mademoiselle Hortense. Beauty and riches were not enough. The Cardinal, dying among his lace-edged pillows, would admit that to himself, realist that he was.

'I must . . . think of it.'

'Remember, in your thoughts, that de Meilleraye is the great-nephew of Cardinal Richelieu.' Both men's eyes turned to the scarlet-robed portrait on the wall, from which the cool grey glance of the man who had forged modern France stared out.

'It is . . . true. Perhaps it is the wisest course. I had wanted Hortense to be a queen.

It is a pity I refused Charles Stuart. Yet who could foresee what would happen?'

'Who indeed? And so may young Armand de Meilleraye live in hope of his desire being granted?'

'Maybe. I will send word.'

'I shall be in Paris four days,' said the Bishop, and took his leave.

* * *

After he had gone Mazarin lay thinking, in almost the clarity of mind he had used to summon before pain clouded his intellect and became the consuming factor, the only truth, in his life. Let the little bitch marry de Meilleraye, and the pair jointly inherit his fortune; Christ Himself had been right when He said nothing could be taken out of this world. 'Forgive me, Lord, if I have erred,' the most worldly churchman of the century whispered, alone in his darkened room. 'Forgive your servant . . . and receive his soul.'

Next day he sent for Hortense and told her that she was to be married to Armand de la Porte de Meilleraye. 'But his name will be changed,' the weak voice said. 'He will take the name of Duc Mazarin.'

'De Mazarin, my uncle?' She wore

apple-green; its garish colour came to torment his eyes where they lay accustomed to half-dark.

'No,' he said, 'the prefix 'de' denotes French nobility. We are not such, but the children of an Italian slum.'

'My uncle!'

'Never forget it. It would not have done for the King of France to marry Marie, or Olympe either. We have what we hold, and must struggle to keep it against the most fiercely entrenched aristocracy in the world. Remember that, and do not fritter away what you will come to possess. There may ensue a time when you are dependent on charity, and that is a hard thing.'

'Surely never, uncle . . . with your fortune . . . '

'It depends how you use it,' he said humorously. The fact that his humour still functioned through great pain touched her; she knelt, and kissed his ring.

'I will marry as you say, my uncle,' she breathed. For moments she lifted her lovely face to contemplate his skeletal one, a study of life against death. Then she rose and, curtseying, left the room with its memories and shadows, and made her way out to where her coach waited. Armand de Meilleraye . . . how odd to have him always about! But she could have done worse.

Armand de la Porte de Meilleraye and Hortense Mancini were married privately in the Cardinal's presence on the last day of February, 1661. Society hardly noticed the wedding; a son had been born to Queen Marie-Thérèse, a child with fair hair, and he seemed destined to live; the King had deserted Madame Henriette d'Orléans for one of her maids in waiting, Louise de la Vallière. It all made gossip the more diverting, and as the Cardinal chose to die ten days after his niece's wedding, there was the certainty of twenty-eight million livres, and the Place Mazarin, with all its treasures, for the couple. Happy Duc Mazarin, as he was now known! Happy Duchesse Hortense! Soon, when other things were dispensed with, one would call on the newlyweds, as was prudent. An early caller in any case had been Marie Mancini, the bride's sister, who was said to have cursed the pair in the Italian of the gutter and to have prophesied that Hortense would be even more wretched than she.

7

The old Duc de la Meilleraye had written a letter to Cardinal Mazarin some time before the latter's death. It read, 'Do not entrust my son with large sums of money.' For whatever reason, the dying man ignored the warning. Hortense and Armand found themselves as rich as anyone in France.

At first, Hortense kept large sums of gold in a cupboard, and invited Olympe and Marie and Marianne and even Philippe to come and help themselves whenever they felt the need. Once the three — Philippe, Marianne, and Hortense herself — amused themselves by flinging handfuls of gold out of the window to watch the servants scramble for them in the courtyard. The story became a scandal; and there were others.

Hortense had felt no surprise at the demands of the married state. On her wedding night, the strained face and loose lips of Armand lay above her, rubbing against her neck, cheeks, mouth, breasts, while his body underwent the violent jerking of a man who copulates; she watched it, half diverted, as if it were happening to someone else. When it happened again she felt his violence, and that her flesh would be bruised; and again, and again, as if he could not have enough of her. 'Do not grip me so hard!' she cried at last, seeing the beads of sweat stand out on his face; it were as though he were in a fit, as though his possession of her were the beginning and the end of everything in life; as though nothing else mattered; as though there would be no tomorrow. Tomorrow came, however, and Hortense was stiff and sore; and by no means pleased when he laid her on the bed again at midday.

She tried to make other things matter in their life together; she gave parties. At one of these the King himself was so greatly dazzled by her beauty that he forsook Olympe, whose society he now generally sought in the absence of that of Marie or La Vallière, and talked with Hortense for a large part of the evening. There was also M Rohan, who paid her much attention. When the company had gone she found Armand furious, almost insane. He dismissed her maid, stripped off her clothes himself, and lay with her forcefully till the candles flickered out in their sconces.

'I am Mazarin,' he breathed against her. 'You shall not mock me.'

'Nobody is mocking you; what has happened

to you? It was a pleasant gathering, and now you have to be as you are. Do not thrust in me so hard; it hurts me.'

'By God, if you play the whore with Louis or Rohan or any other you shall be hurt, no doubt of that.'

'No one was playing the whore with Louis or Rohan. How could I, in a roomful of guests?' She felt an inclination to giggle; she could not take him as seriously as he wanted to be taken. Perhaps love was so, and he had after all loved her for five years. One must make allowances. She let him finish without goading him, and drew away to sleep. Yet he was not done with her, on other nights any more than this; another time he blamed her for having an affair with the Chevalier de Rohan, who had called at the house several times. When she denied it he went into a frenzy; raped her, if so single-hearted a desire could achieve the name, and beat her with his fists; later, when she slept, he got up again, running round the room lighting candles, calling for the servants, shouting that evil spirits were in the room. 'You have brought them here!' he called to Hortense, who kept her long lashes on her cheeks as if in sleep. 'You, you have helped her raise them!' he accused the servants, who bore the screams and curses as servants everywhere will.

8

Marie was by now married to the Colonna, having arrived to a blaze of torchlight and carnival. She took no interest in her bridegroom and went through the wedding ceremony as if repeating a part in a play. Next day 'I was surprised to find her a virgin,' the Colonna announced complacently to the world at large. In all of their brief and unsavoury life together, if Marie forgave him anything, she would not forgive him that.

She had left behind an Italian eunuch who, as a boy, had had a hopeful voice. Unfortunately when he had lost his manhood for it, it deteriorated, and he was out of a profession; he had entered Marie's service as a lackey. When she went to Rome he could not bear to return there, and so she bequeathed him to Hortense. Immediately, Mazarin enlisted him as a spy.

'You must watch and report to me everything she does,' he said, 'especially when she is with the King.' He looked the Italian and up and down. 'I am going to banish all of your sort from Paris,' he said, and stalked off.

The Italian wasted no time in going to Louis; none of Hortense's servants respected her husband. The calm red-brown gaze fastened itself on the speaker; the face, already losing youth, was impassive. Suddenly Louis smiled to himself; he owed Armand Mazarin a large sum of money.

'If what you say is true,' he told the man, 'then he is mad — but although he is the heir of Cardinal Mazarin, he is powerless.'

Mazarin became dissatisfied with the Italian soon, as he did with all the servants, and dismissed him. Instead, he engaged a lady from Provence named Madame de Ruz; also, from old days, Madame de Venel. That pair, he thought, if he thought clearly about anything, should keep Hortense in the pattern of behaviour that was his due as her husband. If he had known, Madame de Ruz and Hortense took to one another immediately; Hortense had been feeling miserable, as she had discovered one final inconvenience of marriage; pregnancy. It would be months before she would be free of the swelling burden, free to dance again and do as she pleased. Why had she permitted her uncle to marry her to Armand? Another husband would have shown more restraint.

Madame de Ruz was a natural mimic. She kept her mistress rolling with laughter as she imitated the Count de Lauzun, with his red nose, and Monsieur, now, alas, the abomination he had feared he would have to become; and the Queen, silent as a tub, imbibing chocolate; and Mademoiselle de la Vallière, the King's latest conquest, who was a quiet modest girl and blushed and wept at the least public notice. 'Imitate a lunatic,' said Hortense, and Madame de Ruz did this so well that the pair devised a further performance to get rid of Madame de Venel, whom they both disliked. Madame de Ruz excelled herself, rolling her eyes to show the whites, pulling down her mouth, and screaming, so that Madame de Venel scurried off down the passage and, shortly, out of the house; she was not seen again.

There was little to do. Hortense played children's games with her servants — Blind Man's Buff was a favourite — went for carriage-drives to meet the fashionable world, played cards with Philippe, who was not an expert cheat, or with the valets. Once or twice she ventured to the theatre. Mazarin immediately forbade everything of the kind. 'You spend far too little time at your prayers,' he told her. 'It is sinful to sit up late, and driving out and gambling are crimes.' His eyes bulged; he was rapidly losing what wits he had. Hortense still made the mistake of deferring to him to keep his calm. 'How would you have me live, then?' she said. 'Praying, and no more?'

He did not answer. He walked to the window, jerked aside the curtain, and surveyed the strollers below. Presently he dropped the curtain and turned back to her. 'Knowing how dear you are to me I cannot be too careful.'

'That is very charming of you.'

'I had not finished speaking,' he said with dignity, adding, 'whatever sport may be made of me, I shall try to hinder your being maligned, because I love you more than my own reputation.'

Hortense shrugged; he must have heard, somehow, of the King's opinion. It was at this time that she fell back, *faute de mieux*, on the company of Philippe and Marianne and, since they were not permitted cards, cast money from the windows. This drove Mazarin almost out of his mind, and he forbade the premises to his wife's brother and sister. Henceforth Hortense was alone; and hedged about with so may restrictions she could hardly move or breathe freely. What were the things she must not do? She must not sit down to a meal with a man; she must not play cards for money. She was to receive no foreigners or Huguenots (this last weighed on her little, as she knew few of either). 'The English lords have designs on the sanctity of my home,' Mazarin added. 'I have instructed the porters to turn them away.'

What kind of life was this, in the heart of Paris? It was almost a relief when, though she was well pregnant, Mazarin announced that she must travel with him into Alsace. The roads were rough and pot-holed and every jolt brought fear of a miscarriage; to be alone in a coach with Mazarin, in such conditions, almost drove her mad herself. Miraculously, there were no accidents, and when they reached a house in the region Mazarin fancied, he took it for several months. Hortense spent the short intervening weeks watching the Alsatian rain fall down on the dreary lurching country; she was nearly eaten up with boredom, and her body was so huge they could not lace her stays. Relief came at the due date, the pains started but were not long or too severe, and the white-capped women told her at last that she had given birth to a healthy little daughter. May she not be as mad as her father, Hortense remembered praying. The child would be called Marie-Charlotte.

9

Hortense was filled with joy at the thought of returning to Paris. The baby thrived with its nurse, who would accompany them; often Hortense would look at the tiny head in its lace bonnet and hope that she herself would not be like poor Mamma, who had had so many children, and worried over all of them. How she would enjoy herself when she saw the gables of the Louvre again! How many parties she would attend now that Mazarin appeared to have regained his reason! How many new gowns she would have made, all in the latest fashion! There would be cards and dancing and carriage-drives and company; the best company in the world, for no other capital boasted such wit as Paris. It did not strike her as curious that she herself should have adopted it as her own native city, as the Cardinal had done; as Marianne also by now had done, for she had become the Duchess of Bouillon and would be another source of invitations, parties . . .

On the day before starting out, Hortense felt sick in the morning. Next day it was no better; a certain fear assailed her; not *that* again, so soon!

But it was true. She did not tell Mazarin lest he forbid her return home. Her eyes would have filled with tears had she let them; to spend nine months, again, carrying an increasing burden, lacing less and less till one looked like a frog, full-bellied! She glanced at her husband's averted profile in the coach; his lips were moving slightly and he was talking to himself. To have to go on bearing children year after year to that creature, that madman! Who else could be expected to endure it? Yet she had done so, and with good nature, and now, as a result, a second child was on the way far too soon. In future one must be short-tempered.

★ ★ ★

She found Paris little changed; and was able to undertake a few of the treats she had promised herself, before her state became known. Gossip was rife; the King, while still fathering children by La Vallière, had turned his attentions partly to war and partly, the last in secret, to Madame de Montespan, who had pursued him with the cunning of the weasel and by now was a raving beauty, with her brown hair dyed blonde, which became

66

her admirably. 'But nobody must speak of it,' said Marianne, worldly-wise, 'because of the Church. It is adultery, when all is said, and even the King cannot be free of the ban if it is discovered.'

Hortense listened, stealthily eyeing herself in a gilded mirror that hung well placed for viewing oneself from the chair in which she sat. The word discovery repelled her; Mazarin had found out about the child, and seemed to be having seraphic visions. Perhaps they would be more peaceful than the demonic ones from which he had suffered on the previous occasion. At any rate she herself looked her best, her skin clear and white, lips and cheeks rosy, eyes sparkling, hair — she never followed fashions with her hair — cascading down her back like a schoolgirl's which became her, she knew.

'What are you primping at?' said Marianne.

'At myself.'

'You are honest. But you were always honest, Hortense. I think that that is why our uncle preferred you to any of us.'

* * *

Mazarin's visions persisted; he obtained a private interview with the King, a thing not easy to achieve. When he had Louis to himself he said, 'Sire, the Angel Gabriel says that I am to tell you that you must at once put an end to your relations with Mademoiselle de la Vallière.' He had straightened from his bow, and stood erect, an avenging sprite and guardian of purity. Louis looked at him and said, 'The Angel Gabriel has told *me* to tell *you* that you are mad,' and called for the servants to take the man away. Yet he took no further action, perhaps because he owed Mazarin money and could always borrow more. As for Mazarin, he went home and immediately commanded Hortense once more to leave Paris. Despite her tears and protests, he put her in a coach again, and the second baby was jolted about the country in its mother's womb as had been the first. Again, however, in due course, the birth was easy; and again it was a girl.

10

By the time Hortense was enduring her fourth pregnancy in five years of marriage, she had begun to realise that she could not forever humour Mazarin.

It was not the births; she always recovered from these, radiant and more beautiful than ever, willing to take Paris to her heart; and the children thrived. She must have inherited Mamma's fecundity. No, it was not that; it was other things, things which happened as it were independently of one another, so that there was no reason for the whole. There had been the time Mazarin, realising after some years of ownership that a great many of the Cardinal's matchless antique statues and Renaissance paintings were in the nude, took hammers, axes and chisels, and destroyed them. There was the other time when fire broke out at one of his houses in the country. He ordered the blaze to be allowed to continue as it was the will of God, and beat the servants who were trying to pour water on it and to save such few belongings as they could. It was as though he detested worldly ownership; already he was involved in a multitude of lawsuits, eating up her money and the children's. The Cardinal had intended that they should be the richest couple in France; now it was not so.

Mazarin still watched her with suspicion. If she liked a personal maid too much, the maid was dismissed. If she ordered her coach, the order was countermanded. Hortense took it all with tranquillity; after a few moments, when Mazarin had left the house, she would order her coach again: and servants were easy to obtain. This was just as well, because Mazarin decided that God must dispose their separate callings; he made each member of his household draw a slip of paper from a box, and on it was written the man's or woman's future occupation; valets were turned into coachmen, scullions into footmen, the latter into carriers of coal.

But the worst of all was the fate of the poor little dairymaids, some of whom were suckling foster-children. Mazarin forbade this to be done on Fridays, and also forbade the girls to milk cows any more; this was to be done by men, and during the day the beasts were to wear their udders veiled in cloth. But still there was the question of the dairymaids' dangerous prettiness; he had them all lined up, and forced each girl to have her front teeth drawn.

Hortense endured it all; and was thankful that Mazarin now turned his attention to his own health, which he declared to be bad. 'I shall go,' he said, 'to Bourbon, to take the waters. You will not accompany me; you will go to my father.'

Her spirits rose; she had always liked the canny, spirited old Duc de la Meilleraye, who had never had any illusions about his son. Once with him, in the ancient turreted château, she began to enjoy herself; neighbours with outlandish names called, and asked her back to visit them; the old man entertained in a lively fashion for her sake, in order that she might not be dull: riding out with her himself among the menhirs placed on the heathery moors in days too far back to recall, by a race too old to name. She loved the strange land, the sunsets over the Channel — was it true this land had once been joined with England, so that the knights of Lyonesse rode to and fro? — and the wayside shrines; her idle devotion stirred and she would slip from the saddle and kneel by them, seeing the face of the carven tortured Christ, perhaps joined by women in stiff head-dresses unchanged since Brittany was a duchy.

71

It was not to last. Bitterly, Mazarin wrote from Bourbon; if she was heartless enough to enjoy herself without his company, while he was enduring great discomfort, she must join him.

'I will write him a letter,' said the old Duc, eyes wise beneath his thinning grey hair; wigs were not much worn in Brittany. 'I will tell him that it is inadvisable to sleep with you while his treatment continues. That will make him wary. He dislikes spending money unless he can enjoy all its benefits.' He smiled at her, and she kissed his hand; if only she could have had such a father! 'I remember,' she said, 'that before my betrothal you wrote to my uncle, warning him about Armand. Would God he had listened to you!'

'Love is strange,' said the old man. 'I love you as a daughter, but I do not love him as a son.'

But it was useless; Mazarin insisted on her joining him at Bourbon. With a heavy heart, Hortense left beloved Brittany behind and set out for the watering-place.

She had reason for heaviness. Mazarin took a large dose of the purifying waters every day, with eventual relief into a series of chamber-pots. She was made to sit in the same room while he pissed repeatedly; the only diversion was the sight of one servant after another coming in with a fresh pot. 'You will come with me to my estates after this,' Armand told her. He seemed, she reflected, to choose the most God-forsaken places on earth to prevent any gaiety invading their souls. He himself had never known any, but hers had been abundant, till now.

During the pissing-sessions she used to examine herself, as one might do before going to confession. Was she too outspoken? The King, who always sought her company because she amused him, had been taken aback at something heedless she had said; she could not remember what it was. 'See that *you* do not talk so,' he had instructed Mademoiselle de la Vallière, and meek Louise had accepted the rebuke which was not hers. I am not a civilised being, thought Hortense. If I were, I would long ago have torn apart the curtains of this room and escaped through the window, leaving him to his piddle-pots. Perhaps one day —

But to leave one's husband was the worst crime of all. Incest — they had already accused her of it with Philippe, because a dividing door existed between the Paris house and the Palais Nevers, which with his new title he occupied, and the brother and sister could exchange visits — sodomy,

73

in which many of the Court from Monsieur down indulged; women's affairs with women, which were so common even Madame was accused of having one with the Princesse de Monaco; unnatural relations . . .

She blushed. Armand himself had once or twice had these with her and she had no way of denying him. At least it would not end in a pregnancy. That, and all the previous things, were tolerated, if coldly; one did not mention them. But to leave Armand would be social suicide. No great house, no royal palace, would ever receive her again.

She drifted away from the thought of that to the memory of the occasional *coitus per anum*, about which she had consulted Philippe. He had laughed. 'We all know it's better from the back,' he had said, 'but nobody except yourself, my dear Hortense, would come out with it like a child at its first confessional. Be more discreet in what you say, not what you do — nobody asks that.'

And so she sat here, while Duc Mazarin passed water.

11

She had pondered the fate of the dairymaids and the art-collection. What might Mazarin do now to the children and herself? If the latter were out of his sight he might forget them; accordingly, as soon as they returned to Paris, she gathered the little creatures together and sent them with their nurse into the country. 'Do not send any word to their father,' she whispered, 'only to me.' The woman nodded; she could not write, but had a good understanding. Hortense turned back into the empty house. Mazarin was out for the time; if he came in and asked for the children, she had resolved to know nothing. Her next child was on the way, causing her to thicken; but one could always drape a fold of velvet or distract the eye with a jewelled belt fastened at the shoulder, in the German fashion. She went to her room, to distract herself, and called for her maid to bring such jewellery as she commonly wore. She tried the belt effect, with some little success; one might set a trend at Court. She smiled into the mirror; there was still pleasure in life.

'You are smiling because of your sins,'

came Mazarin's voice from the door; she had not heard him enter. She replied lightly, good-humouredly, as she always did; Olympe said it was a mistake and she should throw things at him.

'And what are my sins? Tell me of them.' Anything to get him to talk, to keep away from the subject of the children and their nurse; they must be well out of town by now.

Mazarin stalked into the room, so that the light from the window fell on his face. Heavens, how haggard he is! she thought. He had never been handsome, but now it was as if the mind's disease were eating away his very flesh. His answer fell coldly in the room.

'You have committed incest with your brother, and adultery with the King.'

Hortense contained the bubble of laughter that threatened, despite everything, to answer him in its own way. Philippe and she were close, but that was not incest; and, God knew, she had enough of all that with Mazarin to keep her from wanting lovers. Moreover, the notion of a love affair with Louis was bizarre. Perhaps it was because he and she had known one another since childhood, and he had always been her friend. One did not suddenly turn a friend into a lover. I should have Montespan's claws at my eyes if I achieved it, she thought, and unpinned the jewellery and bade her maid take it away.

★ ★ ★

Mazarin harped on the theme that she was the King's mistress and Philippe's, so much so that one night, when Philippe had come to her through the little door, they burst out laughing together at the recital of it. Their laughter had been too loud, and Mazarin stormed in. At once he started carping at Philippe. The latter laughed more loudly than ever. 'You should see a doctor, Mazarin,' he said. 'You are mad.'

'Oh, you are so subtle, Duc de Nevers, you who were trained by the Jesuits! You have a ready answer for everything.'

'The Jesuits did not teach me to sleep with my own sister. Come, good-brother, it is time you took a holiday again. Come to Nevers, where I will entertain you.' He winked over the other's shoulder at Hortense; she took it to mean that she might come if she wished, or stay if not. But Armand whipped round. 'She must come,' he said. 'She must come. I will not let her out of my sight. If I go and leave her here, it will be to find the King in my bed when I return.'

Philippe stood regarding him, his three-cornered smile and tall dark slimness making his seem like one of the irreplaceable early Apollos Mazarin had destroyed. Hortense broke in, to resolve the dilemma. 'I must pack my gowns again; God knows they have had little respite from being trundled hither and thither. I will follow you both to Nevers, as it is your fancy.'

She saw them go off, and regretfully instructed the maid to fold all her newly-ironed gowns again, her laces and chemises; she would wear her hooded cloak on the journey. 'Leave that one,' she said suddenly, surveying an amber-coloured velvet that admirably became her flawless skin and rich hair. 'I will make my farewells in it at Court.'

She went to Court, with Mazarin safely on his journey, and saw what she had expected to see; Louis at cards, with Madame de Montespan at the same table, playing for high stakes. 'Stand behind me, Madame la Duchesse Mazarin, and then I will win,' commanded the King. So doing, and watching idly, she considered him as a physical animal; the erect back, the body athletic from much exercise in his morning gymnasium and his hunting-forests; the great wig that by now replaced his natural, curling, godlike hair; his beautiful hands, which dealt the cards with expertise, as he did everything. 'If you are bad at something, do not do it at all,' was one of his sayings. Why had she never considered such a man as her lover, striven to outwit the Montespan? She could not think of it now; he was not for her. She caught the eye of little Monsieur at an adjoining table; he nodded in friendly fashion. It was a lifetime since he had adored her, had had to have her at his side constantly.

The game was finished. 'You are silent, Duchesse Mazarin,' said the King. 'I told you you would make me win and you have done so.'

She smiled. 'I did not want to interrupt the play, Sire.'

'But the play is over, for the time.'

La Montespan fixed baleful eyes on her. She is pregnant as I am, thought Hortense: How will they contrive that birth? Will they pretend the child is the husband's? The last to have been heard of the Marquis de Montespan was that he had driven through the streets of Paris with stag's horns, cuckold's horns, perched on his coach. Perhaps, Hortense decided whimsically, she should have caused Armand to do the same. She had been too faithful, too subservient.

She took advantage of the lull in the play and bent and whispered to the King. 'Sire, we are all departed for Nevers; my brother with my husband in one coach, I shortly in another.'

'Divert yourselves. There are comedians in most places,' said the King, who missed nothing. He did not turn his head and Hortense made her curtsy and withdrew from the salon. The thought of the coming journey made her head ache. If only there could be a little peace!

* * *

She had travelled half-way along the mud-rutted roads when she met Philippe and Armand returning in their coach. Philippe jumped out, bowed, and said to her 'Turn about, good sister. We are going back to Paris after all. Mazarin has changed his mind. We are going to his country house, not mine.'

* * *

Once at Mazarin's house — it had not been heated or aired, and damp was everywhere — Mazarin caused a fire to be lit with sodden logs and, over its smouldering failure, rated the brother and sister again for what he said was their *affaire*. Philippe suddenly lost his temper.

'Control yourself. Hortense is the loveliest woman at Court. I myself have paid tribute to her in verse, as you know. She could beckon any man to come and be her lover, and she does not; she remains faithful to a fool like you. You owe her gratitude, not abuse.'

Mazarin turned away and began mumbling. Olympe was right, Hortense thought, in that a spirited reply would quieten him; but she herself disliked making scenes, and would rather wrap her inner self away from what was happening outside, keep herself inviolate. At any rate this matter was settled; after a damp and uncomfortable night here, they could all return to Paris.

12

There was a change in Mazarin. Whereas before he had been gloom-possessed, as if accompanied always by guilt, now he was jocular; it was as if some titanic jest amused him from which she was shut out. She began to be afraid; where other women would have cried out in terror years ago, she had let herself feel pity; now there was none. He was eating away her youth, her life; she had not even her children to console her. There was nobody but Philippe, and Mazarin had by now discovered the door through the wall to the Palais Nevers. He had said nothing, keeping it to himself; but she knew that he knew.

He went about during the day with a reflective, facetious smile on his face; she could hardly bear to be near him. Another thing was that he offended her fastidiousness; unlike most women, she had always kept herself scrupulously clean, bathing daily. Mazarin seemed soiled, in particular since the chamber-pot episodes at Bourbon and his perverted relations with her. She would sooner be rid of him than anything else in the world; more and more she reflected on running away, taking whatever consequences came; they could not be worse than her present life. Marianne was kind to her, but what of that? She could not live all her life in her sister's house. Philippe . . . any relations she had with him now would be whispered about, no doubt were already being so, as once there had been whispers about Madame, Henrietta of England, and Louis himself. As for Olympe, she only wanted to placate Mazarin because she could still borrow from him. Hortense had never had any illusions about Olympe.

So . . . she must plan it alone. A jolt came to her at a party at the Louvre, when she was seated among pleasant company, including the Duc de Rocquelaure. She saw Mazarin turn from the King's party, where he had been, and, mincing across the salon like a pervert, smiling terribly, he came to where she sat. The conversation died; he was like a blight, she decided, which brought death or destruction wherever it came.

'Madame,' he drawled, 'I have good news for you. The King has just now commanded me to go into Alsace. You will accompany me.'

De Rocquelaure stood up. 'This is no way to break such news to a lady of your rank!'

he exclaimed angrily. The others, whispering what they had felt for years, wondered how much longer the beautiful Hortense could endure the monster to whom she was married. They watched her rise, and go to the King; tears trembled in her dark eyes like diamonds.

Louis was in good company, affable and entertained. When he saw the Duchesse Mazarin approach he was a trifle bored. These Italians, with their eternal marital problems! One married and endured it, and that was that. Was he himself any better off?

'Madame la Duchesse?' he enquired, thin brows raised. She dropped her deepest curtsy, the brocaded folds of her skirts billowing out like sails round her. He saw her bent, white neck, with the schoolgirlish hair fallen apart at the nape, blue-black as summer grapes. Well, she was beautiful; his mood mellowed, and he put out a hand to raise Hortense. 'In what way can I aid you?' he said gently. A tear brimmed over and spilled down her cheek.

'Sire, my husband has just informed me that you have commanded him to go to Alsace, and he insists that I go with him.' If he knew, she thought, of the dreary months listening to the rain!

'I will not take away his governorships,' said the King. He smiled suddenly. 'You yourself need not stay longer than three months.'

Three months! She would be dead, and there was the child coming! Suddenly, at that moment, in front of the King and the target of all curious eyes, she made up her mind what she must do. 'It shall be as you say, Sire,' she replied, then curtsied again, with even more grace than before; then suddenly flung her head back to meet that haughty, coveted glance. No, she could never have gone to bed with the King. La Vallière and La Montespan might do as they would. She withdrew, and rejoined her own company; and for the rest of that evening was in the wildest spirits. How long would it be before she could again enjoy the wit, the beauty, the *cachet* of the Louvre? Not for long . . . if she became a runaway wife.

★ ★ ★

First of all she made her appearance at Marianne's house; it was not unknown for her to stay there. 'I am leaving him,' she said to her sister when they were together. 'Tell no one, or the plan is ruined. Tomorrow, when he is out, I will go and fetch my jewels.

They will keep me for a time.'

'My poor Hortense, it is sad for you!' Marianne de Bouillon had removed herself, with a happy marriage, from the company of those who might really understand the unfortunate; but she would do what she could. She said nothing when Hortense went next evening to the Palais Mazarin. Its master was in bed, already asleep.

Presently Hortense burst into the Hôtel Nevers, face ashen. 'They are gone! He has taken them. He says they are in Alsace. I do not believe it. I think he has sold them to meet his own debts. I have nothing, Philippe, nothing but the small jewels I constantly wear. And the poor children . . . and Mazarin's lawsuits . . . and the beautiful statues and pictures all ruined . . . ' She began to cry, with a deep welling sound as if the tears had been kept thrust down for long time.

Philippe went to her and took her in his arms. 'We will send for Marianne,' he said. 'We must all see what can be done in this . . . this knavery. By God, they erred when they chose you such a husband! Have no fear, my Hortense, you still have friends.'

Marianne arrived, a little impatient; she had been having her hair dressed prior to going out to mutual friends. 'You are well enough served since you have suffered so much already without saying a word,' she answered sharply. 'You had best come home with me; I will cancel my engagement. I have a friend who can perhaps deal with your Mazarin for you.'

But Madame de Bellinzani, bold as a lion and second to none, was refused admission by Armand. 'Then there is only Olympe,' said Marianne desperately. 'He will see her, or rather the King will; your only help can in any case best come from that quarter.'

But Louis proved to be at his most smug, and lectured Hortense for leaving her husband. 'I see that his friends are my enemies!' Hortense flashed out suddenly, and was dismissed by a flicker of those whip-thin brows.

She braved the Hôtel Mazarin again; after that scene at Court, nothing could hurt her. She sent her groom of the chambers before her, to confront Mazarin. The man returned, crestfallen.

'Madame la Duchesse, he would only say, 'Who are you? Who has sent you?', as though he himself had not seen me a thousand times.'

'I will go myself,' said Hortense.

Wrapping her cloak about her like a soldier, she entered her own house. Mazarin, seeming taller than ever, was standing at the foot of the great staircase, almost posing there. Whatever she said to him was greeted by the new, terrifying smile. Finally she tried to push past him, and they struggled, she in fear that her ankle might be sprained or broken on the step's edge. But she fought with all her might, surprised at how strong she proved to be. Yet she could not pass him, and finally fled down the stairs again and out of the house, with Mazarin yelling to the servants, 'Shut all the doors! Shut all the doors!' No one obeyed him. Her cloak spinning out behind her with the wind and speed, Hortense reached Philippe's house again by the front entrance.

'Some wine, my sister,' said Philippe calmly, seating her in a chair near the fire where the tears of vexation could dry on her cheeks. 'There is nothing better for you now; that, and a good night's sleep. Tomorrow you shall write to the King.'

★ ★ ★

She wrote. Mazarin's activities meantime surpassed his performance at Bourbon. He ordered a young man to come and give him a daily clyster, to clear the bowels.

But before this could be done the young man must go to a priest and make a daily confession. 'Otherwise,' said Mazarin with conviction, 'your sins would enter my body.'

13

King Louis had about him two men he trusted, honest Colbert and suave Louvois. The former had been a legacy from Cardinal Mazarin, so to keep the matter impersonal he sent for the latter. Louvois read Hortense's letter with as grave a face as he might have assumed had the news of the nation been disastrous.

He raised his head, and returned the letter to his master. 'Your Majesty would wish for my opinion?'

'It is the reason why I sent for you.'

'Then I will presume to give it. I think Madame la Duchesse Mazarin is in the greatest peril from a madman. Anyone who could destroy the matchless Mazarin collection would not hesitate, did the mood take him, for a woman's weak flesh.'

'Then what is to be done with her? She cannot live apart from her husband and remain a member of society.'

'Let her retire to some convent — there are many suitable — till the Duc Mazarin is quieter. Her absence may have that effect. When all is said, he has been passionately in love with her since she was a child. It is possible that her very presence brings on these attacks.'

'That is unfortunate for Madame la Duchesse,' said Louis drily. 'I will consider it.' He always gave such answers now, preferring to make up his mind on reflection after an adviser had departed. Nevertheless he knew the advice was good, at any rate the best that could be given, and in due course a letter arrived for Hortense, with the King's seal. She opened it and gave a little cry.

'He wants to put me back in a convent again, as though I were a child! Have I not had enough of restraint? When am I to lead a free life, like others? Do they want me to kill my husband, or myself?'

'No, or you will end like the women in England who are beaten because they have run away from a beating,' said Olympe unsympathetically. 'I myself will call on Mazarin, and see what can be done.'

She went, in a great sweep of fur cloak, her hair dressed high, exuding a heavy scent. An hour later she returned, triumph on her face; a smile played about the painted lips.

'He will be reconciled to you; oh, yes; but on one condition, from which I could not move him. Philippe must go away. He must return to Italy.'

Hortense burst into tears. 'Why should poor Philippe leave Paris, which he loves as much as I do? He will be without distractions in Italy. Remember how bored Marie is there, and she has her own court, and — '

'Well, he can go to Marie and help to enliven her court. It is the only answer, Hortense. You do not want the world to believe what Mazarin has been saying about you and your brother, do you? Then acquiesce in his departure — for a little while. He will be back, you will see.'

Hortense's tear-reddened eyes had narrowed suddenly. 'You want Philippe to go,' she said clearly. 'You want to be able to borrow money from Mazarin unhindered, so that you may attract the King with fine clothing.'

'Very well, you little serpent, if that is all the gratitude you show I will do no more.' Olympe went to a mirror and carefully put her finger on a place on her upper lip; she had been right, a dark down was growing there. One must be constantly watchful; except for Hortense, who continued to wear her beauty like a flower, untended. Would the daily bath she took benefit one similarly? It might be tried, and then —

'I will go back to him,' said Hortense suddenly. 'It may be as you say, and Philippe may be able to return soon . . . or may refuse to leave at all. So many things can happen. Mazarin changes his mind like a child, and perhaps he should be treated like one.'

A child does not indulge in perversions with his wife, thought Olympe; but kept silent. She saw Hortense go out into the night, where torches were lit already.

★ ★ ★

Hortense entered her own house as if it was strange. She found that she had to clench her fists against her bodice to persist in her resolve; never before had she been so greatly afraid. This was a madman to whom she was going, and of all people she was the last he should see. His attack on her might take any form. She must be ready.

· But he was quiet, and left her alone; and this frightened her as much as anything. He might have been a polite stranger with whom she shared rooms at an inn. Even the ghastly smile had gone; the talk was all of courtesy. 'It is a fine day today, Madame, is it not? Our journey to Alsace should be pleasant and easy.'

The child will be born there, she thought. My life is a pattern of jolting back and forth with him, pregnant always. He has never asked about the other children. That means he knows where they are. He can keep silence when he will.

Terror gripped her during the days, the nights; Mazarin never came near her. On the day before they were due to leave Hortense had made up her mind; she was not going with him. She would not travel anywhere with him, ever again, while she lived. To be a social outcast was bad, but not so much as this constant fear, and the changing moods, the silences. Surely in the world there were friends to be met, wit and laughter outside Paris, painters and poets like the little man with the great hook nose who had lately written some tales for her at Court . . . What was his name? Jean de la Fontaine. Why did her mind scamper over notions, remembrances? It should be fixed and steady, and in a way was so. She would leave tonight, and would not return.

★ ★ ★

Olympe received her in a peignoir of white satin trimmed with swansdown. Her long hair was loose and she was preparing for bed. The Comte de Soissons, less assiduous than Mazarin, was out. Olympe shrugged her shoulders, which were beginning to grow

94

more than ever heavy.

'If you will not go with him, then you will not. I will see him if he comes. I am not afraid of him.'

Within the hour, Mazarin came. 'I have come to fetch my wife,' he said. His eyes were glittering, like a lizard's. Olympe smiled pleasantly; the offending down had been removed. 'She will not see you,' she said.

He stamped his foot, as they did at the theatre in high drama. 'What does this mean?' The wronged husband, acting his part. Perhaps all his life he had been acting a part. She remembered that at one time there had been talk of marrying him to Marie instead of Hortense; that at least would have been over sooner.

She lifted her chin, speaking slowly as if to a child. 'It means that she will not go to Alsace, and demands the return of her great jewels.'

'Those have already been sent into Alsace for safe keeping.'

He opened his loose mouth as if to speak further, spread out his hands, scratched his cheek, and suddenly turned and went. Olympe sent for a servant to ensure that Mazarin returned to his own house. The man came in later to say that he had done so.

Olympe went to Hortense, who sat

trembling in a room they had given her. 'He has gone,' she said. 'Now you must await the King's further orders. There is nothing else to be done.'

'Except that I will not return to Mazarin. I *will not*.'

'Wait till the King sends,' replied Olympe smoothly.

★ ★ ★

That happened soon. Swarthy, loyal Colbert, Intendant of Finance, had taken the matter into his hands, which was as much as to say it was in charge of an efficient machine. Orders were sent to Alsace; Madame Mazarin's great jewels were to be brought back and placed in Colbert's care. Madame herself, during her husband's absence, was to be immured in the convent of Chelles.

Hortense wept afresh. 'Chelles! Our aunt is the Abbess and will watch everything I do. I might as well be dead. And after Mazarin returns, what then? Nothing is any better than it was. But I will not go back to him, I *will not*.'

'Console yourself,' said Olympe drily. 'There is another young woman — you met her years ago, when you were both children newly come to France. She has only been able to endure her marriage for a matter of weeks. You are not the most unfortunate person in the world.'

Hortense brightened slightly. 'Her name? I do not remember her.'

'Her name was Sidonie de Lénancourt. She is now the Marquise de Courcelles. She is at St Marie de la Bastille, which is stricter by far than Chelles. Consider yourself fortunate.'

14

Chelles was not too oppressive, for upon her arrival Hortense was sent for at once by the Abbess, her aunt; and having regaled that lady with the variety of her marital sufferings was no longer treated as a prisoner, but as an honoured guest. 'In fact,' said the Abbess, 'you may entertain a little; be discreet, naturally. It would not do if everyone conceived the notion that a convent is a place to receive friends and exchange gossip.'

So Hortense took her at her word and, in the parlour, played hostess to all the variety of people she had met at Court. First of all came Philippe. He kissed her warmly, held her away from him and said, 'No matter what happens, you bloom like a rose. The world of Paris is empty lacking you. Even the Court is dull.'

'That I do not believe, with the King and Montespan making assignations with one another in La Vallière's house to avoid the gossip.'

'You have heard of that? It is cruel.'

'As for you, should you not be in Italy?'

'If one waits long enough, biding one's time, certain things are forgotten. Do the same, Hortense. We shall see you back at Court yet.'

'Not until Mazarin has undone himself by some means, and entered a monastery.'

'My poor Hortense! He is mad, quite mad, and the King knows it. But Louis owes him money.'

'How do you come across these subtleties, unless you listen at doors?'

'Nothing is secret, if one has patience.' Philippe overrated himself, she thought; but how good it was to see him! He was dressed finely, and his eyes devoured her as though he were her lover. That was what Mazarin thought, she reminded herself. It was not often that she herself let her thoughts drift in the direction which they did on her brother's departure.

'Be careful, Philippe! Be careful!'

She entertained other guests, mostly women of her own age or a little older, full of gossip about the King; more and more he was becoming a sun surrounded by obedient planets. 'When this palace of his is finished at Versailles, we shall all have to go and live there; nobody will come to the Louvre, or even to Paris, any more,' lisped Mademoiselle de Montalais, who was about to be married: she had been Louise de la Vallière's friend. But one did not ask about Louise. It was whispered that she talked of going into a convent. Well, if it is one like this she will not do so badly, thought Hortense.

Her thoughts were shattered by a letter which came a few days later.

Mazarin had seen the King. He had complained that his wife was being encouraged to receive visitors, not all of them female; one of them, indeed, her brother Philippe. He asked that Hortense be removed, for the sake of propriety, to St Marie de la Bastille without delay.

★ ★ ★

She was escorted there by a party of guards. The first thing she saw was the dread fortress from which the convent took its name, rearing under a dark sky. There were rumours of men and women who had spent a lifetime there under *lettres de cachet*, and had never come out. Perhaps she was fortunate. Shivering a little, she allowed herself to be helped down from the saddle and ushered into the Abbess' parlour, which was less friendly by far than that at Chelles.

'You will conduct yourself as others here,' she was told. 'There will be no visiting. This is a strictly enclosed order, and we allow no laxity.'

The Abbess' pale hand then beckoned an attendant nun. 'You will escort the Duchesse to her cell and see that she makes the acquaintance of Madame la Marquise de Courcelles,' she was told. Hortense followed the nun out into a long flagged corridor; it was damp and cold. How could women live out their whole lives here, and would she be condemned to do so unless she returned to Mazarin?

'Madame la Duchesse Mazarin. Madame la Marquise de Courcelles.'

The other was a rogue, with a mischievous pretty face. After the nun had gone she whispered, 'I am glad to have a companion; before, it was like the cold pit of hell. Why are you here?'

'I left my husband. Why are you?'

'I left mine, after three weeks. I prefer my lover, the Marquis de Cavoy. One day I hope to see him again, but I cannot carry out my plan unless I have someone to help me. Will you?'

'Gladly, if it will ease *ennui*.' Hortense had taken a fancy to this engaging little person; she could not be seventeen years old, and yet had had the resolution to achieve what she, Hortense, should have done long before. Why, she had never taken a lover, or thought till lately of leaving her husband! At least now she was not alone in the world. 'What are we to do?' she said.

'First, we must send for a pair of lap-dogs.'

'I have none. Can you provide one for me?'

'No doubt. Mine is called Fifi and the other has no name, for she was born of a mongrel mating. She is ugly, and can bark, and that is what we want; we must leave these sisters no peace until they get rid of us.' Sidonie de Courcelles grinned, showing wide-spaced teeth. Hortense started to laugh; the creature was diverting, and she had not been diverted for a long time. 'I shall call her Nounou,' she said. 'It was my mother's pet name as a child, and my uncle called her by it all his days.'

'Your uncle was Cardinal Mazarin.' Sidonie's eyes narrowed.

'Indeed so, but he is dead.' She spared time to wonder how the Cardinal would have acted had he known that his favourite niece was confined first in one convent, now in another.

★ ★ ★

The little lap-dogs arrived and after initial shyness, like novices, they set up a happy barking. Hortense and Sidonie teased and tickled them, chased them along the corridors, and made them happy while the nuns were made miserable. At nights Nounou and Fifi slept on their mistresses' beds; as they could not get out, they made puddles and messes which the lay-sisters were left to clean up.

Once Mazarin appeared. Hortense happened to be wearing patches on her face, and he said he could not endure it and it troubled his conscience.

'You are right, he is mad,' said Stéphanie de Courcelles when he had gone. 'What you must have endured! And you are pregnant again, you say?'

'It is tenacious. Whatever happens to me, I seem to give birth to living children.'

'It will be worse than the lap-dogs. We must hasten, if we are to succeed in our plan,' said Sidonie heartlessly.

★ ★ ★

The plan was ruthless. There were rats in the convent, as in any old building, and Sidonie and Hortense enjoyed rat-hunts, cheering on

Fifi and Nounou with loud huntsmen's cries, generally in the middle of the night, or when a particular hour of silence was enjoyed by the convent's Order. They waged a silent war also; they emptied the holy water stoups at the entrance to the chapel, and filled them with ink; devout sisters entering and crossing themselves with a drop or two on their fingers got their habits ruined, spotted with the stuff which would only turn brown with washing, and never be washed out. As for any ink-pots in the convent, the two girls filled them up with water; this effect was not so dire, but it all helped. Confusion reigned in what had formerly been an orderly, strict place; when a stern word was said to Sidonie and Hortense they raised innocent eyes and asked for water to wash their feet. Hortense could not have her daily bath here; there were no facilities, a fact she did not hesitate to point out. At night, after the nuns had gone to bed exhausted by their daily routine, the two young demons overturned the receptacles which had held the water, ensuring that wet dripping through the ceiling would disturb the sisters' sleep. Other charming little tricks were tried, and succeeded; in the end the Abbess sent for the pair. They stood before her expressionlessly, Hortense thickened with her child, the other lean as a monkey. Neither showed any sign of contrition.

'You have made our lives here, which were peaceful, intolerable. I could wish that you had not been sent to us. My only course, apart from complaining to higher sources when I can, is to set certain sisters of ripe years and sensible ways to be with you constantly.'

Sidonie nudged Hortense as soon as they were out of the parlour. 'Did you hear what she said about higher sources?' she hissed. 'The façade is cracking. I think we would have made good soldiers.'

The group of prescribed sisters had assembled before they reached the end of the passage; thereafter the girls were followed wherever they went. Fifi and Nounou still barked cheerfully; the girls ran at top speed, racing along the narrow passages and through the hitherto inviolable rooms; it might have been a hunt, with the fox leading the hounds. The poor old nuns, who never took excercise, found the going hard. Their habits were heavy and consisted of many layers, worn by the years to felt; they sweated and panted, but still must run on; Mother Abbess had ordered that the two young women were to be kept in sight, and kept in sight they would be. Out to the cloisters the girls ran, Fifi and

Nounou yelping alongside; a cry from behind did not stop them, but one poor old nun had sprained her ankle.

'Do not stop to pity any of them,' whispered Sidonie. 'They cannot keep this up for long.'

But they kept it up for three months, to the exhaustion of everybody; Hortense's child was almost due. By now, every member of the convent was aching and ill; of all the penances that had ever been prescribed, that of guarding these two young women was the worst. Better a thousand years in Purgatory than another month of this! So the nuns murmured to one another, and in the end went to the Abbess, to beg that the two girls might be sent elsewhere.

The Abbess gave a grim smile. 'They are determined to be sent back to Chelles, and I suppose they may as well go; better that than ruining our health and peace.'

So Hortense and Sidonie were escorted back to Chelles, and the Abbess there, Hortense's aunt, had a hard task to keep from laughing when she heard all about what had happened at Sainte-Marie.

So they were back, and shared a cell together. After the portess had passed by with her lantern Sidonie reached across from beneath her thin blanket and touched

Hortense where she lay awake.

'Now we must leave France,' whispered the undefeated young woman. 'I have made all our plans. Wait till the morning.'

★ ★ ★

However, before this could happen Mazarin came, with permission from the Archbishop of Paris, whom he had stormed with words, to take Hortense away from Chelles and to bring sixty horsemen with which to do it. The Abbess, a redoubtable lady, confronted him through the entry-grille.

'What do you want?' she said.

'My wife, the Duchesse Mazarin. By the laws of God you cannot keep her from me. I have permission from the Archbishop to break down the door and take her, if you will not give her to me.'

His wild expression and dilated eyes reaffirmed the Abbess' opinion of him from Hortense's tales. She told him calmly, 'I am in charge here and I have the keys. This door was built many hundreds of years ago and has withstood worse shocks than you propose inflicting on it. I can complain to the Archbishop of your disorderly conduct if you so much as strike one blow at this enclosed place. I bid you good day, Duc Mazarin.'

The grille slammed shut, and presently it opened again with Hortense's lovely face behind it. 'I am the Abbess now,' she giggled. 'My aunt has given me the keys.'

'You will open the door and let me take you away at once.'

'I will not. As I said, I am Abbess while I hold the keys. I will not come back to you. I do not like you. There is no entry for you here but by my favour. Go away; I do not wish to see you, now or ever again.'

Mazarin withdrew, his lips chumbling, saying, 'I will return tonight. I will return tonight.'

'The answer will be the same then,' replied Hortense, and shot the grille home. On returning the keys to the Abbess she said 'You have seen him now, and know what he is like. Why did they marry me to him? Why?'

'My child, the ways of God are strange,' said the Abbess gently.

★ ★ ★

Night fell, and the two trembling young women waited in suspense, holding one another's hands. 'I do not want your horrible husband to take you away, Hortense,' said Sidonie. 'We have been happy together. I

108

wish we could be so always.'

'Listen . . . it is the sound of horsemen. My husband has come back. He will storm the convent, as he said.'

'Do not be afraid. I know where we will go. There is a wide chimney we can climb. Once we are on the roof we can traverse others; I've seen it done. Then we can go to your sister Olympe at the Hôtel Soissons; it is not far.'

Whether or not Olympe would welcome two soot-smeared vagabonds was doubtful; but Hortense was so greatly afraid of being returned to Mazarin that she did not dissent from the plan. Sidonie, still the soldier, went first, climbing until she came to a grille. 'It is narrow here,' she called back. Hortense followed, and wriggled through the grille to her waist; after that came the pregnancy, and it would not let her through. Sounds of hammering came dimly from below; her terror increased; how could they fail to capture her, stuck here? 'Help me, Sidonie!'

Sidonie pulled. Hortense seized her bunched skirts and tried to stuff them upwards through the grille, forcing her stoutened body to follow. It took twenty minutes of torment to free herself from the grille. This child surely would not be born alive. She felt tears run down her face amid the caked soot as she stepped out at last on to the rooftop; it was steep and the dark Bastille loomed near.

'I cannot look down,' she whispered in fear to Sidonie. 'If I do I shall fall.'

But Sidonie had already started to laugh. 'Friends have come!' she panted, holding her blackened hand to her breast to aid her breath. 'It is not Mazarin! It is our friends! Let us climb down and greet them!'

And climb down they did, to be lifted up in the saddles by young men known to them, known to Marianne, known to Olympe. 'We came to assure you of our support, black ladies,' said one. The girls were laughing so much that it infected everyone in the court; great gales of masculine laughter came from the young men on horseback.

'Good fortune, Hortense! Good fortune, Sidonie! Be assured that if any should attempt to force you to do what you do not want, we are here; only send us a messenger, and we will band together and come.'

⋆ ⋆ ⋆

In fact, it was some of these same young men who heard Hortense's suit in the Court of Requests and decided that her jewels must be returned by Mazarin. 'He must refund what he has spent out of her dowry, also,' called some, while the rest applauded; by the end, Hortense had received the right to live alone at the Palais Mazarin and to receive twenty thousand livres a year, while Mazarin himself must live elsewhere.

So she went home. It was paradise to find the great house warmed and cheerful, with no gloomy marital presence to make her unhappy and forlorn. She turned her head aside from the ruined statues and slashed paintings; that was over, and could not be helped. She turned to her maid, Nanon, who was waiting to take her cloak and unlace her out of her street-dress. 'Nanon,' she said, 'warm me a bath. That is all I want; and that will be heaven.'

'I too,' said Sidonie.

15

All that Hortense needed was peace before the imminent birth of the child, but Mazarin left her none. When the decision of the Chamber of Requests was made in her favour, the Duc proceeded to the Great Chamber, which was by no means made up of young men; the old diehards in it even disapproved of foreigners, and the memory of Cardinal Mazarin was to them anathema. They had no hesitation in rescinding the edict of the former court, and informed Mazarin that he must occupy the Palais with his wife and resume his marital authority.

This news came to Hortense when she was in labour. She could not have told afterwards which she felt most strongly, rage or pain; but thankfully, as always, the birth proved easy for her, and in due course her son, scarlet as a boiled lobster, lay in the crook of her arm. She looked down at him and tried to prise open the tiny fist with a finger. When had she had any joy of her children? Would not other women now, even peasant women, be rejoicing with their husbands beside them, and a first-born son? But for her, there was only bitterness; and as soon as might be this little creature — she had decided to call him Paul-Jules — must join his sisters in the country, safe from the bickerings of his father and mother and the everlasting upheavals of their lives.

'Why have you decided on Paul-Jules?' asked Sidonie, leaning over to admire the baby. She had stayed on at the Palais Mazarin, partly because she liked Hortense and partly — this had been her difficulty from the beginning — she had no money of her own at all. Here life was comfortable, for as long as it lasted. But Sidonie had not forgotten her plans for leaving France with her friend, if the worst came to the worst.

Hortense answered dreamily, and yawned with desire to sleep. 'Because although I love my brother Philippe, he is too wicked a man to name my child. My cousin Paul is a monk and therefore good. And Jules is for my uncle, who after all left me everything.'

And Paul-Jules, who had survived climbing up a chimney, racing through a convent, and numberless emotional upsets while he was being fashioned, slept, and his mother slept by him.

★ ★ ★

113

The King intervened; he had heard of the birth, and had some sympathy for Hortense although he could not afford to approve of her conduct. He ordered Mazarin to keep to his own part of the Palais, with his own servants, and not trouble his wife; nor was Hortense to be forced to travel on journeys with him. As for the money, Colbert and Louvois would administer it between them. Louis dismissed the matter from his mind, had his favourite horse saddled and rode in company to inspect the progress of building at Versailles, which he loved increasingly and made plans for whenever no other business occupied his attention.

16

Hortense had never confused reality with dreams. Now, for the first time, it began to be difficult to separate what had happened from the known world and the world of nightmare; even to remember whether or not Paul-Jules had then been born. There had been a time when, secure in the fancied knowledge that half the house was her own, she had begun to entertain a little; she had noticed that there were certain refusals, but shrugged if off; the diehards would no longer receive her or in that case, she them. She took pleasure in arranging little supper-parties, grand receptions, even a theatre; she had engaged players who would act a comedy before an invited audience refreshed with fruit-flavoured ices. On the night she had dressed, she remembered, with diamonds in her hair, and worn a lowcut gown. Her breasts were beautiful, why not display them? And the glances of admiration from the male guests proved her right, and cheered her. The fiddles from the hired orchestra had struck up and everyone was in their place, chattering in low voices before the curtain should rise;

then suddenly Mazarin rushed in, tore down the curtains, revealing confused players not ready to be seen, and screaming, 'This is a saint's day. It is profanity to have this entertainment here. Everyone must leave. I forbid it! I forbid it!'

Such things would add to her own toll of scandal, already made obvious when she had visited the Louvre with Olympe. The King did not receive her smiling as was his wont; he kept his eyes fixed on his hand of cards, uttered a cold little speech, and went on with the game. She was valueless, now, as a queen of Parisian society; she should have known it. But what harm had she done anyone in face of the harm which had been done her?

At this point Sidonie left, saying she would return to her husband. She knows which way the wind's blowing, Hortense thought. A few days later she was passing the Courcelles house and saw, outside, the coach belonging to the Marquis de Cavoy, Sidonie's supposed lover. A kind of fury enveloped Hortense. Was the whole world false? As she stood there, saying she knew not what, Courcelles himself came out, and said a strange thing.

'Madame la Duchesse, I myself have always been in love with *you*.'

Nightmare again, and Courcelles and Cavoy making passes with drawn swords to satisfy one another's honour, their full white shirt-sleeves blown in the little breeze that came fitfully across the flat place where they stood. Afterwards, Hortense heard the lie that Courcelles had spread about herself. 'She is a make-weight,' he had said. 'She will have throats cut for her if she can.' In fact, he was jealous of Hortense's friendship with his wife; but that was over.

* * *

Mazarin himself was giving out that they had resumed marital relationships, which they had not. She never wanted to have him touch her again; she saw to it that even their meals were separate. She had the baby sent away early, fearing harm to him.

It was at this time that she learned that Mazarin was bringing a second set of requests to the Great Chamber, asking for full restoration of marital rights. Something snapped in Hortense's brain. She could not go on living here; she must get away, leave France, go where Mazarin and his councils had no power over her any more.

17

Philippe, of course, was her first adviser. They discussed ways and means of travelling to the Italian frontier, where Marie would receive them, and suddenly Philippe looked at Hortense gravely and said, 'Do not tell Olympe one single word of this, or we are betrayed.'

'Betrayed? By Olympe? But she is our sister.'

'That means nothing since you, my dear, inherited the Mazarin fortune. Olympe, as we all know, has been eager to dip her fingers into it. How often have you lent her money, or seen it returned? Now her source of supply will be cut off, which she will not like. Be careful.'

'Philippe, Philippe, I feel surrounded by enemies and betrayers with but one friend; yourself. If you too are false, I think I shall kill myself.'

'You will not; you have too much love of living. In any case you know well I am not false. Have I ever given Mazarin a single instance of the rumours he has put about concerning us? I have not even troubled to deny them; I have remained your friend.'

She had blushed, remembering the charges of incest. 'Yet our uncle always said you were wicked,' she murmured. He smiled, while the corners of his eyes seemed to lift, like a devil's.

'Ah, that. I do not think myself any less wicked than he. Did you ever know that, having called in as libellous all the early pamphlets about the Mazarinettes — you, Marie, Olympe, Laura, the cousins — he had them reprinted some years later at his own cost and sold them for a fortune? That is what our uncle was like, Hortense; and yet he was not a wholly bad man. No doubt all of us are a judicious mixture of both. But you, my poor child, are more of an angel than most of us, and life has dealt with you hardly. Yet there is one debt you owe Olympe; one she will not forget or forgive.'

'What is that? I owe Olympe nothing.'

'You owe her your beauty, which has not diminished but has rather increased with the years. Olympe soon will be a middle-aged woman; she is growing heavy, her chin is double, her marriage is wretched, her eyes no longer sparkle to lure the King or anyone else. She is a jealous, prying woman, and she will spoil your plan if she may. Give me your promise that, no matter how fair her manner may seem, you will breathe not a word of it to her.'

'I promise.' He kissed her, and went; their escape was planned for the sixteenth of June. He and she would leave Paris by different routes, then join one another on the way to the south.

18

They were to leave at eleven, when the summer daylight had begun to fail. It was still only four o'clock. Hortense lay on a couch unlaced, dressed only in an easy, full shift which reached to her ankles and had sleeves gathered into a heavy lace frill at the wrists. She had lain fingering her long hair for some moments, then had taken up her lute which she liked to play at idle times, and strummed on it. There was no particular melody, only the pleasant strumming and plangency; it passed the time, and kept her from thinking. She did not want to think, or remember; there had been a scene with Mazarin yesterday. He had come upon her in one of his violent moods, and she had threatened to summon the servants to protect her; upon which he had burst into wild laughter. Hortense could no longer forbear shouting, 'I will leave you, I will leave you,' and on a sudden he had stopped his laughter and grimly, like a judge, said, 'You would not dare.'

She had begun to be frightened; he must

on no account suspect the plan. She had smiled, and spoken calmly. 'I would run so fast, Mazarin, that if you spend your life pursuing me you would never catch me.'

'You have not the courage,' he said, and walked away.

She did not want to think of that, or remember any of the other things she was running away from; King Louis a friend no more, and acquaintances cutting her in the streets, all because of the affairs at Chelles and Sainte-Marie, and the renewed turmoil with Mazarin. For some time now she had gone out little, amusing herself with Nounou, the little dog Sidonie had left behind, or with the lute. She let her fingers twang at the latter, slowly and more slowly; she was drowsy and almost asleep.

The door opened; it was the maid, Nanon, who would come with them tonight. She looked scared, as she had done ever since hearing about the plan. Nevertheless she would not have opened the door had it been Mazarin. 'It is the Comtesse de Soissons, madame.'

Olympe stood in the doorway. Philippe is right, Hortense thought; she is growing heavy, and is no longer handsome. She stayed where she was and let the visitor walk into the room. As always, Olympe looked about her critically.

'Why are you dressed like this, at such a time of day? Why do you not go out and be seen about town? It is no use hiding here; people will say you have reasons for being afraid to be seen.'

'They may say what they choose.' A long chord, like the wind in branches, came from the lute. 'Put that thing down,' said Olympe irritably. 'You should be thinking how best to placate the old men of the Chamber, that the verdict may go for you. You were never sensible of your own good, any more than Marie.'

'Marie does not trouble you now.' An arpeggio of separate notes; then Hortense laid the lute down gently. 'What do you want with me?' she asked, as if to a stranger. Money again, no doubt, she thought; but she can sing for it.

'At least have yourself dressed, and come with me to Court at St Germain.'

'You must excuse me.' It was the only safe saying; Philippe had advised her on it. Olympe gave a little sound of disdain and began to pat at her carefully dressed hair in the mirror. While she did so, another caller was announced; a friend and ally of Philippe's. How unfortunate that the two

123

should have met! Fortunately there were certain code words, which made little sense to another listener; the man used them, Hortense gave her answer in them; it was about the various routes to be taken. The visitor bowed and withdrew.

'Who was that idiot?' enquired Olympe. 'Anyone would think the rumours were true, and you were planning to escape to Italy.'

'I shall stay here. You must excuse me.'

'Very well, little parrot; I am going, as I see I'm not welcome. I still think you should come to Court tonight. I will send a messenger, in case you have changed your mind. Be sensible, Hortense!'

She had gone; standing just for an instant in the doorway of the room, so that the light was behind her. Seen thus, she had a quality that made Hortense shiver suddenly; what could it be? She herself was not given to imaginings of evil, though there had been enough of it in her life to prepare her. But Olympe looked now, for instances, like the woman she would become, who in her middle years and old age would be accused of witchcraft, poisoning, and murder, all for gold.

She turned and went.

★ ★ ★

124

Later her messenger came. The summons was curt; Hortense was to meet her sister without fail at St Germains. 'Tell the Comtesse that I shall meet her there after dinner, not later than ten o'clock,' said Hortense. One had to tell lies. Soon there was a knocking at the door and it was Philippe.

'Are you ready?' She told him of Olympe's message. 'If I meet her,' he said, 'I will know what to say.'

On the outskirts of the city, the Nevers coach was stopped by that of the Comte de Soissons. Olympe wound down the window and leaned forward. 'Where is Hortense?' she said suspiciously. She and Philippe had never been allies.

He affected surprise. 'Have you not seen her?' he exclaimed. 'Then she must have taken the other road to St Germain, for I saw her leave.'

They drove on, one in doubt, the other with certainty.

19

Two odd male characters might have been glimpsed riding out of Paris in a rocking *calèche* that night, its bulk mercifully concealing their shapes beneath the fashionably short coats. Hortense's plump, enticing behind did not go with breeches, and as for Nanon, the maid, she had knock knees and big breasts to hide; moreover neither could keep on their periwigs, which were perched atop piled hair neither woman had had the heart to cut.

They had won so far, and were almost out of the city, when Hortense suddenly gave a little cry and said, 'Mother of God, Nanon, the jewels! The only jewels I have left, that *he* has not taken! I have left them behind at the Palais. We must return.'

'Madame, madame, they will capture us,' wailed Nanon, who was beginning to wish she had never agreed to come on this adventure. But one would do anything for Madame la Duchesse. Hastening the coach they regained the house, slipped inside, met nobody — by a miracle, Mazarin himself was not at home — pocketed the jewels quickly, and fled. They were on the road again, none the worse except for being a little late, within half an hour, perhaps less.

'This *Calèche* is intolerable. Can you ride a horse, Nanon? I intend to find one as soon as may be, but Paris isn't safe; we must wait to get to Bar, which is far enough away for us not to be known.'

Fortunately Nanon had been reared on a farm, and could ride, if not very dexterously; and the horses they were able to hire at Bar were sound enough. After this they made more speed, and for the first time in her life Hortense watched from her place in the saddle the dawn breaking over Nancy. Its glowing colours meant hope. A new life was beginning, even though she did not know where it would end. After all, who knew where they would end in any case?

'The Duke of Lorraine is my friend, Nanon. He may well have a message for me here.' And this in fact proved to be the case; Charles of Lorraine, whom Marie Mancini had once half-heartedly offered to marry, had not forgotten her beleaguered sister. Hortense tore open the sealed letter eagerly.

'Madame, madame, what is it? Is it good news?'

'If you are going to continue to call me

madame we had best change back into our petticoats. The dear Duke invites me to stay with him. I dare not, for Mazarin you may be sure is not far behind us; and in that case, Charles of Lorraine offers me twenty horsemen to escort me to the Swiss frontier. There is a friend!'

'May we indeed put on our petticoats again, madame? I feel at present that I am not a respectable woman.'

Hortense burst out laughing. 'Yes, yes, but wait till we find an inn across the frontier. There we may dress, and comb out our hair, and be ourselves again. But it has been a jest, has it not?'

'Madame, madame, you would laugh on the brink of hell!'

★ ★ ★

The escort was waiting, and beyond, in the clearing dawn light, the heights of the Vosges which they must in the end circumvent. She was glad of the men riding on either side of her; to have been overtaken by her husband's agents here would not have been pleasant. At last she felt the free air of Franche-Comté on her face, and turned, glowing, to thank the captain of the troupe.

'I owe my safety, perhaps my life, to you

128

and to your master. Thank him many times, and more thanks to yourself and your men. If I had money I would give it them, but, alas! I have only enough for our journey.'

The captain refused gallantly, saluted her, and watched her ride out of sight. He would always remember her beautiful face, flushed by the light of morning.

★ ★ ★

Philippe met the women here as arranged, with his valet Couberville and Hortense's old admirer, de Rohan. Having eaten at an inn and changed into a riding-gown and broad hat, she felt more herself again; so much so that she eyed de Rohan, decided that it was a good thing she had not taken him for her lover, and let her gaze linger on the valet instead. He was not unhandsome, solid, well-muscled and with a set of the eyes and lips that showed he would be a good man to have in danger. Hortense found the sight pleasant after the memory of Mazarin. Pray God she need never set eyes on him again!

Philippe de Nevers had been glancing behind them once or twice. 'I think,' he said, 'that at the next inn we come to, you had best change back into men's attire, though I know you do not like it. We are, I

129

think, being followed from a distance. When we come to the inn, Couberville and Rohan and I will keep questioners occupied, while you change your garments. They will have been instructed to look for two ladies; if there are none, well, that is that.'

So they toiled upstairs at the next inn and donned the ugly periwigs again and their breeches and short coats. By now, having met Philippe and seen handsome Couberville, Hortense was in tearing spirits; when they got outside she started to chase Nanon round the innyard. It was cobbled, and she tripped on a projecting stone and fell, giving a cry of pain. Philippe started towards her, but Couberville was there first; his strong arms lifted her easily: the absurd periwig fell off and her blue-black hair, shining, scented, fell loose and heavily across his coat.

'What have you done to yourself, madame? Where does it hurt?' His voice was very deep and, to her surprise, bore little accent; it might have had a trace of Gascon. 'Oh, my knee, my knee,' she moaned. They carried her inside the inn and fetched hot water and dressings, and washed the knee. But soon it swelled so greatly that she could not ride. 'We must put you in a litter,' said Philippe, biting his lips. 'This is no place to stay in safety; we will try to gain Neuchâtel, and you may rest there.'

* * *

'There, my little one, there. That is the place where it hurts, is it not? Let me rub it for you with warm oil. Yes, it is painful, but it will grow better now.'

She set her teeth, clenching her grasp against the bevelled edges of the inn-couch on which she lay, closing her eyes against the pain. When she opened them, it was to see Couberville's sunburnt neck bent over the top of his white shirt, and above that again his dark, lightly curling hair. His ears were small and close-set. How strong his hands were! They had pummelled and stroked and rubbed and massaged her swollen knee, which at one time had been in danger of turning gangrenous, while she lay here in an inn, miserably contemplating a return to Paris. How could a cripple ride abroad? And they would have had to cut off the leg. Couberville had saved her from that. Daily, twice daily, constantly, he had come, and had given her exquisite pain, but it was better now; even with the ugly bruised flesh showing yellow and green and violet still, it was growing better.

'Bend the leg now, madame, and straighten it again. Yes, it will hurt. That is good; try again.' But she broke down and sobbed and said that it hurt too much; that would do for today; she wanted to rest it. 'If you rest it too much, it will stiffen,' said Couberville grimly.

'Then I will try once more — once more — ah, the pain! Do you remember when I wept by the hour and said we could not go on?' She was white with the effort, and lay still.

He raised his face and grinned at her. 'I remember. Your tears wet my shirts while I held you against me, telling you not to be a little fool. You shall not go back again. From now on, we will go forward; soon you shall be in a litter once more, and after that on a horse.'

Her eyes never left him. 'One thing would give me courage, Chevalier.'

'You call me that.' He flushed. 'I am only a servant, no more.'

'Three generations ago my ancestors tilled the soil in Sicily. I am no better than you.'

'That is not for me to say. I live only to carry out your wishes.'

'Do you? You swear it?'

'Name a wish, and I will try to carry it out;

132

but I am not God, who can do anything.'

'You can do this thing. Chevalier, I want you to make love to me.'

★ ★ ★

After their passion she lay satisfied as a cat, not moving her hurt knee lest it spoil the sensation she had of total fulfilment. She had been dissatisfied, not at first knowing why, for the past weeks; then she had realised that Mazarin, with his assiduous forced lovemaking, had accustomed her body to it, as a starving man will yearn for strange food even though he dislikes it. Now, the food was wholesome, tender, sweet. They had not spoken, merely lying with their lips in contact, caressing with their hands, he very gentle lest he inadvertently touch the hurt knee; beyond her satisfaction was amazement that a man should be so tender. With Mazarin she had never known tenderness: he had taken her roughly, furiously; she closed her memory against it. Now, she knew; she had experienced the passion that comes to a woman when a man is patient, and she had trembled and seized his arms with her hands and set her mouth against him, while the delicious inward flow came; lying back afterwards, with a sigh of contentment, her eyes closed, smiling.

When she opened her eyes, he had gone.

* * *

Back in Paris, Mazarin had naturally fallen into a passion when he returned home to discover that his wife had fled, taking with her her everyday jewels but not, as it happened, certain passionate poems contrived for her by Philippe, which made the prying husband think the worst, as in fact he had done for years. He rushed straight to the Louvre, where the King was in bed; it was in fact two in the morning.

Louis received him. The King was one of the few mortals who can maintain dignity in a nightcap, and also he had the faculty of certain soldiers, being able to collect all his wits at once on waking. Thus, he was able to master the trembling, infuriated Duc at a glance.

'It was remiss of the Angel Gabriel not to warn you that your wife was about to run off,' he said smoothly. Mazarin trembled and wept.

'What am I to do?' he asked. 'What will you, Sire, do for me in this matter? Once she is beyond the frontier it is more difficult.'

He felt the bathos of his own words and sank into miserable silence.

The cool royal glance surveyed him. 'I have promised the Duchesse that I will have nothing to do with her concerns, and I shall keep my promise,' said Louis. 'I will now send for the servant to show you out. On another occasion, remember that your King works each day while you lie abed, and be tactful.'

★ ★ ★

Next day Mazarin tried Colbert. Perhaps the lack of high-born blood made the minister a realist; at any rate, he had sympathy with Mazarin. 'Send some person, not unimportant, sympathetic also, after her, to talk to her and persuade her to return on her own terms,' he suggested. 'On no account go yourself; that would make things more difficult to mend.' Colbert sounded rueful; he had just had a serious quarrel with his own wife, to whom he was devoted.

'I will do as you say,' said Mazarin. He went away mumbling to himself, thinking of sympathetic persons he could send.

★ ★ ★

135

The sympathetic person rode at last into Milan, where the Duchess Mazarin had already arrived and had been welcomed by her sister, Marie Princess Colonna. Thereafter Hortense had, evidently, moved into a villa the Colonnas had provided for her, and was at home to nobody but a servant named Couberville.

20

They lay in surcease, her arms about his neck, a finger now and again curling the ready hair; his face was hidden against her breast as though he were her child, and her dark silk mantle of loose hair hid their bodies. In fact, Hortense was thinking less of him, who had grown daily more necessary, than of Marie; what a bitter hard-faced woman had met her at Milan, not even the ghost of the girl whom the King of France had passionately loved! The Colonna had been there also; Hortense had disliked him, but could not show it as he had offered her hospitality. The villa was private, and they would be left here alone, unless Philippe appeared and made himself tiresome. He had returned to France some time ago, to do his devoirs; his marriage contract had been signed with one of the young daughters of Madame de Montespan. He was rising in the world, was Philippe; first Duc de Nevers, and now —

'There is a rider in the courtyard,' murmured Courbeville against her. 'I shall dress myself.'

'Why?'

'Because if you want to see him, I must show him in, and if you do not, I must show him out.'

'Tell him to go away. I will see nobody.'

'As madame says.' He was already scrambling into his breeches and full shirt. When he had gone, she lay looking drowsily at her own body, amazed at its possibilities. It was still beautiful, not yet beginning to put on too much flesh. The triangle of dark hair below her abdomen intrigued her; she put out a hand and stroked it, and then took both hands and cupped her breasts. She had continued the fashion of showing them above her bodice; it was becoming, and drove away bores.

But poor Marie . . .

Courbeville had returned. 'It was a messenger from your husband,' he told her. 'He wanted to speak reasonably with you.'

'I am beyond reason.'

'So I told him. But if the Duc de Nevers comes, madame, you should see him; in fact he will not be kept out.'

'There is no word of his coming back that I know of.'

'Nor I. But come he will, unless I am mistaken; and he will be angry with me.'

She drew him down to her again. 'I will

not let anyone be angry with you, my Chevalier. Do you know that during the past weeks I have been happier than in my whole life? That I owe to you; remember it, and do not be humble.'

21

The news from Paris was better than might have been supposed; the Great Chamber had decided in Hortense's favour regarding the jewels, the money, and her right. Immediately, Mazarin had riposted, with the cunning permitted to the mad, with a series of accusations against his wife; she was having a love affair with de Rohan, another with her brother. The last charge had been a stale joke for years, but this time Mazarin was able to show Philippe's love-poems to Hortense; they proved nothing. 'The highest infamy and lewdness has been perpetrated in my house, under my protection, and continues now wherever they are,' announced Mazarin in the high, piping voice he used for his more infallible statements. To have clapped him up would have been the answer, but the King would not go so far.

Philippe de Nevers took horse and rode indignantly to the Colonna palace, telling the news to Marie and her husband. The three sat in a circle near the brazier, surrounded by baroque and classical objects, half-heartedly drinking wine; when a glance did pass between the Colonna and his wife it was filled with dislike and mistrust. 'We called to see her several times, but she would not receive us,' he said petulantly. 'The servants told us she is entirely taken up with this Couberville.'

'Couberville! I'll have him out of there in moments! Excuse me, Marie, my dear; excuse me, Excellency. I will ride there this minute — no, I am not so weary, your good wine has refreshed me.'

'You will return to sleep here tonight?'

'If I may; it is unlikely that I shall be welcome at the villa. Of all follies! Farewell, then, till later.'

He was gone, and they heard him ride off on a fresh horse Colonna had provided. The silence of coming night settled down; Marie got up from her place and began to move about the room. She was never at ease in the presence of her husband. His eyes followed her for a few moments, resentfully. She had been a bad wife to him; had had a love affair, had gambled away much money, and now had involved him in her family's disgrace. He would be as well rid of her; but the King of France was her protector.

'I am going out,' he said, and flung out into the night. After he had gone Marie crept back to the brazier and warmed herself. So Hortense was in love at last, and with a servant! Now she would know what parting pangs meant! She had always been so carefree before, despite Mazarin. What wretched marriages they had both made! There was the constant presence, stronger lately, of fear. She herself was far from home and had made few friends in Italy. If only she could return to France!

* * *

Philippe burst into the room where the lovers were lying, regardless of the scandalised protests of Nanon, who said her mistress had forbidden any callers whatsoever. She saw his tall cloaked figure stride through the forbidden door, then went to the footman, Narcisse, to gossip about it. Neither of them now liked Couberville, who had begun to give himself airs.

'How dare you come in here!' Hortense sat up, naked; her hair fell partly about her body and she pulled it forward, to make a covering. Couberville was naked also and stood upright, much at a disadvantage; he had no weapon, Philippe was his master, and there was no doubt as to his guilt. 'Get out of here,' said Philippe thickly, 'or I will throw you out of the window.' He came and stood over the man, who was of slightly lesser height than he; he would have carried out his threat, as was evident. Hortense reached for a wrap and cast it about herself, then stood up between the two men, her white feet bare on the tiles. 'Go away,' she said to her brother. 'I will not receive you or anyone. You shall not come to my house and behave as you have done.'

'The house is Colonna's, and he is weary of your conduct. Unless this man returns at once to France I will do as I say; a fine sight he'll make, cut about with glass, lying naked in the street.'

Couberville suddenly turned and knelt to Hortense. 'Do not dismiss me, I beg of you,' he said simply. She could see the adoration in his eyes, like those of a dog. 'I shall be ruined, madame — ruined! Where am I to go? My master will give me no peace till my head is on a scaffold.'

'Do not be foolish,' she said gently. She cast an arm about the man's shoulders and turned to Philippe. 'Have you at least the manners to retire while we dress ourselves?' she said. 'Then we can talk, if you must.'

'I did not come here to talk, but to get rid of that stallion of yours,' said Philippe coarsely. Within himself he was shaken and disturbed by the beauty of Hortense's nakedness. Why should a man not love his sister so? And he loved her dearly, dearly; and she had left his poems in Paris for Mazarin to find and read.

'Go now, till I send,' she said; she suddenly seemed to have taken command. Couberville was embracing her knees, both white as alabaster now that the injury she had taken in Franche-Comté had healed. Philippe turned and went out and Hortense bent down to her lover and said quickly, 'Dress, and keep yourself armed. When he is angry he can be dangerous. Defend yourself if you must.'

'As long as I may stay with you, madame, that is my defence.'

She felt a slight, stirring impatience; nobody but a servant would speak so. 'Do as I say,' she told him, and when he had gone sent for Nanon and made her lace her into a becoming gown, and comb her hair. She would have liked a warm bath with herbs in it; making love made one also sweat, and she liked to feel fresh always; but there was not the time. Dressed, she would be able to talk to Philippe, make him see reason. If he loved her as he said, then surely he would want her to be happy?

He came in and they talked as she had foreseen. She flattered herself that she had conquered him for the time. 'Keep the miserable fellow, if you must!' he flung out at last. 'It cannot be forever; even a fool like you will see him for what he is, in time.'

22

From then on Couberville was miserable except in the arms of his mistress. He felt, and rightly, that the other servants laughed at him behind his back, plotted small humiliations for him; Nanon the maid was worst, because he had never looked at her. Then came Narcisse, the footman whom, had Couberville had any training in classical lore, would have seemed the double of his namesake, entranced with his own parts. These persecutions would not have mattered, but a greater one still came from the Colonnas and Philippe, whom Hortense had brought to see reason, if that were the word, about herself and her lover: Why should she be made unhappy any more? What harm had Couberville done anyone? 'My reputation belongs to myself, and no one else,' she said to an angry Marie Colonna, for the noble couple were still inclined to send Couberville about his business; Hortense replied that if he went, she would follow him. Marie shrugged her shoulders at last and left it alone; Colonna continued to keep watch on the affair. It was he, before Hortense noticed it herself, who received word that she was with child.

This simply would not do. He sent for his wife and rated her as if the pregnancy were her own. 'And if you had proved as fecund as your sister, it would have been a good thing!' he spat. Marie raised her head proudly; she was not easily subjugated by him.

'It is of no use to talk,' she said, 'the thing is done. What are we to do now? She cannot have the child in Milan, where everyone will know and gossip. Of your many estates — ' her tone was bitter — 'there is surely one where we may take her, with Couberville at first for the sake of peace, and then get rid of him and see the child born safely in a convent. I have an aunt who is Abbess of one near Venice.' The Mancini family were rich in aunts who were abbesses.

'We will go to Venice, all of us,' said the Colonna sullenly. 'But I am weary of your relations; they cause nothing but trouble.'

So do I, doubtless, she thought; but did not reply.

★ ★ ★

They travelled to Venice in a cavalcade, the noble Colonna, his wife, his sister-and

147

brother-in-law, and a trail of servants from both households behind. Peasants gathered at the roadsides to see the great ones pass. Hortense sat in a carriage, feeling sick. She knew her state now and merely, in the unreal situation she seemed to be in, recalled that every time she had been pregnant by Mazarin he had jolted her about in carriages, and now the same thing was happening, but not by the wish of poor Couberville, riding behind.

Venice rose out of the mists at last, and they saw green water and, at last, an array of damp palaces; one of these was the Colonna's, and they disembarked and were ushered in to splendour of a damp gilded kind, with the gilt peeling. Hortense walked to the ornate window and looked out; it was as one might have expected, with gondolas on the green water and a gondolier tying up his craft to a gaily decorated pole near the palace. She would explore the city, she thought, with Couberville by her; next day she sent for him. Nanon returned, her face smug.

'He is ill. He says that he has been poisoned by the Duc de Nevers. I do not know anything.'

★ ★ ★

He was lying on the pallet bed that servants use, eyes shadowed, body limp and flat. When he saw her his eyes widened and showed a brilliance of joy. She knelt down by him.

'My poor Chevalier. How is it with you?' She could smell the vomit which had been taken away. He continued to regard her with the brilliant, unearthly eyes.

'It is well with me when you are here. While you are gone I am nothing and will soon be dead. Promise that you will not leave me.'

She stroked his hair. 'I would promise anything to get you well.' She turned to Nanon, who had discreetly lingered near the open door. 'Get me a cup of cool milk,' she said sharply. 'See that no one handles it but yourself.' She turned back to the sick man again; they said he could swallow nothing. 'You will take a little,' she said gently, 'for me? It will make you well.'

'From you, yes.' They stayed as they were, she kneeling on the floor by him, holding his hand. Presently the milk came and as he had promised, he sipped a little as she fed it to him; soon he turned away his head to say that he could take no more. She straightened the cover under which he lay and tried to make his head comfortable with his rolled-up cloak; it was borne in on her that matters like pillows, sheets, feather mattresses, were unknown to servants. She had not thought of it before.

'I am going now,' she said softly, 'and you must sleep. Do not take food unless Nanon brings it to you, or I myself.'

'Bring it to me yourself. Nanon does not like me. None of the other servants give a fig for me since . . . '

She laid a finger on his lips. 'Nanon is trustworthy,' she said. 'I cannot always come. But when I can, I will be with you, as I am now.'

'I have a bad dream in which you have gone away. You will not go? You promise?'

'I promise.' She kissed his forehead, rose, and went out.

★ ★ ★

'You cannot expect to remain indefinitely with your lover in my husband's houses after this scandal. The longer you stay about him, the worse it gets. Leave the wretched man to recover — of course it was nothing to do with Philippe, he merely ate something that disagreed with him. You cannot tie yourself to a servant, Hortense. Mother of God! You and I used to be fond of one another in our

150

childhood — cannot you understand that I am talking to you for your own good?'

'If you only saw him — and he made me promise — '

'He had no right to extract such promises from you. As I say, my husband is growing impatient. He thinks we ought to leave here and go to Rome. The man Couberville cannot travel in his present state. He can be looked after here, and then follow.'

'Marie, Marie, you know what it is to love!'

'I chose the King of France, not a lackey.' Marie flushed and turned away. Hortense watched her thin erect back. Matters had gone hardly for Marie, especially as she was not happy in her marriage. Hortense remembered the time long ago when this sister had stalked into the Mazarin residence and cursed in gutter Italian their respective miseries. Some had come true.

Marie had turned to face her again. She suddenly came over, laid her hands on Hortense's shoulders, and said in a low voice, 'Hortense, I need your help. Do not deny it to me. I am afraid.'

'Of the Colonna?'

'Of his practices. He has got rid, before now, of those whom he no longer needs; and he no longer needs me. I am useless to him; we have never meant anything to one another. That marriage should not have been forced upon me; I would sooner have retired to a convent, as Mamma wished. Is there something evil about me that both my mother and my husband have loathed me and my lover cast me off?' She flung her hands up over her eyes to hide the tears that came. 'Come with us to Rome, Hortense. Do not anger the Colonna any more. Your Couberville will be looked after, I promise.'

'I will come,' said Hortense. But she still reproached herself about the sick man upstairs; she dared not go to him to say goodbye.

* * *

She could not force herself to look at and admire the vista of Rome with the seven churches, the dome of St Peter's showing above the pall of blue mist that covers every city from the distance. She was feeling ill; this pregnancy was telling on her, and it would not be long now till she must retire to the convent for the last months before the birth. One did not embarrass the Colonna by appearing pregnant in his company. She looked at the ungenerous face of her brother-in-law, the embittered face of his wife. Marie had made the worst of a bad marriage. I too, thought Hortense; but I tried to please Mazarin, at the first. Mazarin himself seemed a long way off, part of another world. She hoped devoutly that she might never see him again.

'This is the palace,' said Marie. They had travelled through the city while Hortense thought of other things. Liveried servants hastened to open the great man's coach-door, assist himself and his lady and sister-in-law up the steps. This was a drier, airier, more open, less magnificent shadowed place than the house in Venice. On all sides were windows with *putti* supporting them, and panoramic views. Hortense longed for a bed on which she could lie down. But she had to endure the elaborate meal that followed with its ritual, the food served off gold crested plates; she toyed with it and ate little. Afterwards, she pleaded weariness and made her way to the large room which had been given her; despite her exhaustion she could not sleep. Couberville would know, by now, that she had gone away from him, despite her promise. Surprisingly, she did not long for his embraces; only for peace, to be left in peace. For that night she was granted her wish.

* * *

Next day it was shattered. The spacious hall was filled with company, representatives of great names who had called on the Colonna and his wife, half formal, half curious about the rumours that were flying from city to city concerning the Princess Colonna's sister. Marie's face was like a mask; she received everyone with courtesy but no warmth. The Colonna, as always, was affable and pleased with himself. Hortense was introduced to those bearing names she had heard of or remembered from the early days in Rome; the Orsini, the Manfreducci, the della Rovere. Their men gazed at her dark hair and eyes and provocative breasts, the women noted her toilette and her talk. She enjoyed the last, and was settling down to it among the assembled guests when there was a stir at the door. A man with a pale sick face had come walking unsteadily in as though he were the owner of the palace; it was Couberville. He made his way straight to Hortense and began to shout at her, as though there had been no one present but the pair of them.

'You promised that you would not leave me, and now you have broken your word.' He was livid, almost ready to faint with

154

exhaustion, rage, and illness; she would have liked to comfort him, but dared not. Marie de Colonna came striding over, her silk skirts rustling in the silence that had fallen.

'Go,' she said. 'You will get your deserts in the courtyard.'

'Not unless the Duchesse desires it. I will be commanded by none but her.'

Hortense suddenly flung up her hands in front of her face, and fled towards the stairs. She ran to her room and there told Nanon to let no company in, no, not the mistress of the palace itself. It had been Mazarin all over again; a haggard reproachful face, accusations of broken promises, embarrassments. Downstairs, there had come the sounds of a scuffle, then silence, then the talk broke out again; she could hear it from here.

She did not sleep that night. Next morning, clad in a peignoir, she went to seek Marie.

'What happened to him?'

'What do you expect?' Marie's tone was cold. 'He was arrested for causing a disturbance of the peace, and will spend the next few days in prison till the charge can be brought. You did yourself no good by retiring; there will be talk, despite all I've done to stop it.'

Hortense was not listening. Prison! And he

had been sick and ill. It was true; she had betrayed him. Tears ran down her face. 'I beg of you,' she said, 'have him released. He will die if he is kept in confinement.'

'If that is done, do you promise to have nothing more to do with him? That is the one condition of his freedom.'

She has discussed it already with her unpleasant husband, Hortense thought. She nodded slowly. Couberville in the free air, lacking her, was a less miserable creature than Couberville in a damp dungeon, hoping for a renewal of their love. And it could not be renewed; somehow, it had died, she was not sure when.

'I will not see him again,' she said slowly and sadly. 'But you must set him free.'

'It shall be done,' said the wife of the Colonna.

23

The convent smelt like all other convents, of beeswax, scrubbed tiles, starched linen, and charity. She was conducted to the parlour of the aunt-Abbess, whom she remembered meeting long ago as a child, holding Mamma's hand: and being bidden to remember her prayers and given a rosary. How she had fallen from the standard expected of her! The pursed lips of the Abbess showed no trace of sympathy.

'I must ask you, niece, while you are resident with us, that you cover yourself becomingly; these low-cut bodices will not do. They suit neither your state nor your station.'

'Madame.' She tried to claw together the frail stuff of her shift to hide her breasts; she had grown accustomed to showing them and had forgotten about them. 'I will ask my maid,' she was beginning, for Nanon had come with her and was waiting outside. But the Abbess said coldly, lowering her eyes from the unedifying spectacle of a half-clad, pregnant niece, admitted here for a time by the persuasion of the Princess Colonna,

'What provision do you intend to make for the child?'

'I can make none, madame. I myself have no money and have pawned such jewels as I brought with me to Italy.' This was true, and she could not in any case have continued trespassing on the Colonna's hospitality as a penniless dependent. 'After the child is born, I hope to travel to France and try to obtain an interview with King Louis, to ask that what is due to me may be sent. The courts — '

'That does not concern us. We are concerned with your child.'

'Madame, I have never been able to keep any of my children with me.'

'It sounds as if your affairs have been badly mismanaged by someone, probably yourself. However, as I was about to say, we can find the child a wet-nurse among the peasant women who come to the chapel here. Later, if it is a girl, and you desire this, we can bring her up in a manner conducive to a later vocation. However it will depend on how much money is available to her as a dowry then.'

If there is none, thought Hortense, she will remain a lay-sister, scrubbing and laundering. I do not want that to happen. 'I will do what I may, madame,' she said submissively. The Abbess inclined her head in its stiff wimple and regarded her own hands, red with hard work.

'That is all very well. If the child is a boy, the local priest will help us. But too many children are left to be brought up on charity. It is better if their pleasure-loving parents help with their keep. We cannot afford more than we may. Meantime go to your cell. We will be in the chapel at seven, if you wish to join us; but nobody will force you.'

I had better not show myself until my chemises are pulled together, thought Hortense. She made her curtsy to this evidently disillusioned aunt, and found herself out in the passage, where a novice waited to show her and Nanon where they were to sleep. The latter complained bitterly. 'Cold as winter, madame, and you are accustomed to be kept warm! And there can be no baths here; I have asked.'

Well, we must endure it for as long as it takes, thought Hortense; and at least, behind these enclosed walls, they were protected from attacks by Couberville, even Mazarin. To think that all this came about because we dressed up as men!

She began to laugh, and Nanon stared at her as though she were crazed. She was like a child, Madame la Duchesse; nothing would keep her spirits low for long.

24

After what seemed like a term in prison, the baby was born, put out to nurse, and Hortense escaped back to the Colonnas. They were more civil now that she had got rid both of the embarrassment and of Couberville. He had been set free, she heard, but she would not see him; it was better so. Even Philippe was forgiven, whether or not he had attempted to poison the man. Poison was very fashionable just then; one poisoned old sick relatives for their money, poisoned jealous husbands and nagging wives, poisoned enemies of state. It was not too closely enquired into.

'You will find it,' said Philippe, lazily leaning back at last on the coach-cushions that were to take them into France, 'even at Court — in the most unexpected places. One does not always do it to kill; there are powders to make one sleep, powders for rendering one impotent, other powders that are a strong aphrodisiac. The makers of them grow rich.' Looking at Hortense, he thought that she at least would not need the aphrodisiac; after each birth she seemed to grow more and more beautiful, and admirers had crowded about her during the short stay in Rome and had twice fought duels over miniatures of herself, framed and boxed in silver for snuff, that she had given them. But poor Hortense was in no real state to give anybody anything. 'Do you think the King will allow me my money?' she asked, like a child. 'Do you suppose he will?'

'He must, otherwise we must put you forever in a convent to be free of Mazarin.' But the tears rolled down her face, and he laughed and kissed her; he had only been teasing, he said. 'In my new state I shall be able to slip you something now and then,' he told her, for his coming marriage to Madame de Montespan's daughter would bring him a handsome dowry for her.

They idled over their journey, sightseeing whenever they passed through a place of note, stopping at an inn whenever it served particularly good food. Philippe did this of a purpose, both to regain Hortense's health and to put off his marriage, for which he was not overly anxious, except for the money. They left the route often, to visit châteaux and old bridges and waterfalls, to admire the mighty height of great mountains capped with snow, to brave the cobbles of mediaeval towns. Once they stopped for a fortnight at a village where the sun seemed warmer than anywhere in France; vines grew over the loggias of the houses and good wine made from them was stored in every man's cellar. Philippe and Hortense idled, tasting the wine.

The time passed; they were like lovers on honeymoon, except that he never touched her. As for her, she was content, as she would always be when there was no unhappiness, no anger, no urgency; and Philippe saw to it that she had none of these, and moreover paid for everything. He knew, none better, that Mazarin would be fuming in France over the delay in bringing home his wife that he might scold her. But Mazarin, Philippe had determined, would not get his hands on Hortense again.

All in all, their journey from Rome to Paris took them six months. Mazarin was, understandably, growing impatient, and babbling of incest to whoever was prepared to listen.

25

'My wife? She is the greatest sinner alive. I will not receive her until she has spent two years in a convent repenting of her sins. The world does not seem to realise how delicate I am. In fact I am a tulip. You must place me in the sun and pour water over my head.'

They removed his periwig, placed a towel about his neck, put him in a sunny place and duly poured water. Since the episode of the dairymaids' teeth the servants of Mazarin had shown no surprise at any order he might give or countermand. Now, however, there came a positive edict. A troop of guards and a company of archers were to be ordered to the French frontier to arrest Madame la Duchesse should she attempt to cross it.

Grimly, they rode; they had been told what to do and would be paid for it, a consideration which did not always apply in great households. On reaching the frontier, however, they found opposition; the Provost of the nearest town, having had the news in advance, had called out his own array of men; Hortense would be allowed through or there would be battle fought. The two sides stood glaring at one another; nobody seemed to know quite what to do, and the Duchess's coach was still not in sight.

Fortunately, the King's ear was close to the ground. A courier galloped in, carrying a written order. Mazarin was to sign a truce with his wife and the latter was to be allowed to enter France, and Paris, in safety.

When he heard the news the tulip broke down and watered his own face with tears. 'All men are against me,' he said. 'Even the King is against me.' The troops had all ridden home, and had cost him a great deal of money.

★ ★ ★

In the interests of discretion Hortense and Philippe had parted when they reached Paris, as she had been offered hospitality by the Colberts. It was a relief to be ministered to by kind Madame Colbert, who made no pretence to be an aristocrat and did her own cooking and cured her husband's toothaches. 'I seem to have been journeying for ever, but now I have come home,' Hortense told her. Madame smiled and curtseyed; she had never seen so beautiful a lady; how could the husband be as cruel as they said? Colbert himself kept a discreet silence on it; he knew

164

it would be better if Hortense Mazarin stayed out of France.

★ ★ ★

Hortense had an interview with the King in the apartments of Madame de Montespan, which were by now far easier of access and more commodious than the Queen's. She had been fearful of meeting the King again; but, on rising from her low curtsy and the kissing of his hand, she looked into the red-brown eyes and saw in them compassion, and much more. He knows everything, she thought, for his agents will have told him; he knows about Couberville and the baby, and the duels in Rome, and why we did not hasten back to France, Philippe and I, because we were happy together. Yet he will say nothing of it and will only act on what is important.

'I need not enquire for your health, Duchesse Mazarin, for I never saw you in greater beauty.'

'Your Majesty is kind.'

'As you know, I would have been kinder; but you did not give me the opportunity; and, madame, your conduct has been a weapon in the hands of Mazarin.'

He smiled. 'There are two courses open

to you. Either — and this will be best for you, despite the difficulties — you return to your husband under my protection and support — '

'Never! Never! Not if I must walk a beggar in the streets! You do not know — '

'There is no need for you to be a beggar, and I know very well,' replied Louis drily. 'The alternative — and I daresay you will choose it — is that you return to Italy, where evidently you are happy, and that I make you an allowance of twenty-four thousand livres a year. You may choose, Duchesse Mazarin.'

'Your Majesty is kind. I choose the allowance.'

A buzz of talk broke out from the courtiers. She was as mad as her husband! 'She will,' said someone, 'spend the money in the first inn she comes to, and then what will she do?'

But Hortense told herself that she knew now how to value money. The days of throwing it down in the courtyard for servants to scramble for were over. Many things were over, among them Mazarin.

★ ★ ★

It had taken her six months to reach France; it took nine to get her back to Rome.

Meantime Mazarin was pestering the King. 'It is unheard of to take a wife away from her husband!'

'That depends on how the husband treats his wife.'

'I will send messengers to plead with her.'

'You may do as you choose.'

The messengers arrived, found Hortense the centre of a doting circle of Roman aristocracy, related their instructions, and heard the Duchess laugh and say something in Italian. Suddenly the crowd burst out in a shout of 'No Mazarin! No Mazarin!' to much clapping and laughter.

'It was the war-cry of the Fronde, you understand,' Hortense had explained. 'They did not like my uncle any more than my husband.'

So the messengers rode home.

★ ★ ★

All should have been serene; but Marie de Colonna was in danger. She came one day to visit Hortense and begged that all servants might be dismissed from the room; this having been done, she leaned forward and grasped Hortense's hands, like a drowning woman. She was more haggard even than

167

on Hortense's last visit; the great eyes were dark with fear.

'He will poison me,' she said. 'I am going to leave him before it happens. I helped you when you were desperate and now you must help me.'

'How can I? How — '

'You must come with me, help me on the journey. I dare not take much in the way of money and jewels. I must go to the only place where his power may never reach me again.'

'Where will you go?' But she already knew.

'To France.'

A slow flush spread over Marie's thin cheeks; she rose, turning and turning about the room like an imprisoned animal. Hortense gazed at her frankly and guessed what her sister's thoughts must be; she still saw herself as the young girl who had entranced Louis XIV, and did not realise what the years had made of her; a scraggy, bitter woman whom nobody would look at twice or listen to for longer than moments. 'Do not go there,' said Hortense. 'Everything has altered from our day.' She did not want to hurt Marie, and said no more, but thought of it; Montespan queening it over the Court, La Vallière a humiliated second rival; the change in the King himself from an eager boy to a cool, hard-minded statesman, with etiquette becoming so rigid that soon it would be improper to show any feeling at all. Marie would be unbearably shamed and mocked; she must not go. Yet the face which turned on Hortense over her shoulder held the old obstinacy, the old *esprit*.

'Perhaps not everything. You must accompany me; that will make things easier; you have the *entrée*.'

Hortense spread out her hands despairingly. 'Marie, you do not understand! I banished myself from France when I declined the King's offer of protection if I returned to Mazarin. I dare not cross the frontier.'

'Then come as far as the frontier,' said Marie sullenly. 'You cannot deny me that.'

26

Towards the end of May the Colonna announced that he would go to visit his stud-farms in outlying parts, and would be gone for three days. Hortense and Marie did not look at one another. Their preparations were all made; Marie's passport and papers had been got by the connivance of little Monsieur, once Hortense's inseparable friend when he was a boy of thirteen at the Louvre. Marie had some time since struck up a friendship with his *mignon*, the Chevalier de Lorraine, who was banished from Court, to Monsieur's fury; certain factions were working for his return, but King Louis had been persuaded by Madame Henriette, Monsieur's English wife, that the Chevalier was not to be endured in her house. Meantime there it rested; but Lorraine knew that a grateful Princess Colonna would do him no harm, if the King befriended her as he had done in times past.

The Colonna duly rode off, with his train. As soon as the dust of their going had settled, Marie and Hortense hurried to their respective rooms; Hortense had decided she would leave certain personal effects behind, to divert suspicion. Marie opened her jewel-box and took out some diamonds and only one other thing; the Stuart necklace of pearls King Louis had once put round her neck in the days when he had loved her as he would never love any other woman. She would not part with it whatever became of her or however long she lived.

Their coach drove leisurely out of Rome; nobody would be suspicious at the sight of the Princess going for an early morning drive with her sister, or even at a glimpse of the maid Nanon, hood pulled forward, seated with her back to the horses beside Hortense's groom, Pelletier. The servants were in the plot; it had been arranged that they make for Cività Vecchia, where a boat would be waiting; it was safer by far than going overland, pursued by the Colonna's men.

They had left in the cool dawn, and by the time they reached the ancient port it was dusk; the *felucca* was waiting some way off, its shape clear against the silver sea. 'It will be better to send the coach back now, madame,' murmured Pelletier. 'If we change to horses, it may be noted.'

'They cannot take us on board here?'

'No, they are waiting for us to join them secretly, a little way off.'

'Can we not hire horses for the time?'

'No, we must walk. I will go on ahead to tell the captain we are here; you follow as best you can.'

Marie looked dismayed, for she was idle and had never walked far in her life. Hortense did not mind; she enjoyed walking. As for Nanon, nobody asked her. They began to make their way down a coast path towards a coppice Pelletier had pointed out, which would guide them towards the place where they might take ship, and where he would meet them.

It was growing dark. 'Have we no lantern?' whimpered Marie.

'We must not show our whereabouts.'

'Soon it will be impossible to see. Why could they not have come nearer?'

'Trust Pelletier. He is honest and has been with me now four years. Go carefully, and do not twist your ankle in those shoes.' Marie was wearing silk court slippers, with heels stained red such as every Court copied from France; but they were of no use for covering any greater distance than a palace floor.

Soon it grew quite dark. 'We cannot go on,' said Hortense. 'We must spend the night here, and start again when dawn comes.'

'You speak so lightly of it! What if there are robbers in the wood?'

'We have little for them to take. And the Colonna's agents will not look for us here.'

Nanon listened grimly; trust her lady to revel in an adventure, but the Princess Colonna was another matter. A pampered bitch, was Nanon's private opinion; but she arranged the ladies' cloaks in silence, bunching the hoods to make a pillow of sorts, and tucking the folds round them when they lay down.

'I have never, never in all my life — ' began Marie indignantly. Through the darkness came Hortense's laughter.

'It is an experience. And we are not cold. Listen to the sea lapping! Tomorrow we will be on it, making all sail for France.'

She herself prevaricated slightly, for she was not going to France; the Duke of Savoy had promised her his protection, and she would go there after Marie was seen safely on her journey. She nestled down into the folds of her cloak, and was soon asleep. On waking, the sky was bright with dawn. 'Marie!' she whispered. 'Marie!'

'Oh, you have no need to waken me; I have not slept a wink all night.' The Princess Colonna sat up, smoothed her ruffled hair, and looked with loathing about her at the little sheltering wood.

'Get up,' said Hortense, 'and walk. There

173

will be no breakfast for us till we get there.'
She still sounded gay.

They walked, with Marie's blistered feet
ever less likely to support her. There was
no sign of Pelletier, who should by now
have come to meet them. 'We are betrayed,'
said Marie miserably. 'We must return to
Rome.'

'Return if you will, but I am going on.
Listen! I hear hoofbeats.'

Marie gasped. 'Pelletier left on foot. It is
some robber. We are betrayed, I say; we may
as well give ourselves up.' She fell to dreary
weeping, while Hortense dived into the small
valise Nanon carried, brought out a brace of
pistols, cocked them, and waited with one
in each hand. Marie sank down behind a
half-concealing willow, her hands over her
mouth. Presently she heard Hortense laugh,
and call out to someone.

'You! What are you doing here? Where is
Pelletier? What of the boat?'

The man dismounted, and bowed; he was
one of the postillions they had left with the
coach. 'Madame la Duchesse, I do not trust
that groom. I have hired another, a better
felucca, nearer than the other. I will go back
by the coast road; but you must not, as you
will be seen. Follow that path — ' he pointed
out a winding way between the trees, and

174

gave definite instructions as to how to find the new boat. 'You will be safe soon. Have no fear.'

★ ★ ★

The inland road was winding and dusty. Hortense was happy; she had taken off her shoes and stockings and walked with graceful ease on the hot pressed earth, as her Sicilian ancestors had done generations before. Poor Marie could not so shed her gentility; she staggered along behind her sister, stopping every now and then to rest, having to be returned to and comforted, hauled up again and coaxed to hurry on. The fear was that the boat might sail if they were not espied soon; the other fear was that the Colonna's agents would capture them if they were. Torn between the two fears, Hortense made haste, Marie could not.

Suddenly the ground parted to reveal the sea again, and the shore. Hortense gave a cry of joy. 'It is the sea!' she rejoiced. 'It is the sea!'

There was a moan behind her; Marie had sunk down on the road, her head drooping. Hortense caught sight of a peasant in a field, weeding between his rows of green corn. 'Help us,' she called. 'Carry this lady a little way; she cannot walk further.' The thought of being delayed now, with the sea in sight, was maddening; but Marie could not help herself, let alone anyone else. How different we are, Hortense took time to think; life is harder on her than it can ever be on me.

The peasant was surly, and refused; he had his weeds to clear. Marie, waking to consciousness, offered him a hundred pistoles. At this he came out grudgingly, leaving his hoe dug deep in the soil, and lifted her with ease. They strode along, making better speed now; suddenly, a man's figure appeared. At last, it was Pelletier.

'Where have you been?' called Hortense. 'We have been nearly mad, in great fear lacking you.'

The man fell on his knees, watched by the peasant who set down Marie on the road. 'Forgive me, Madame la Duchesse; it was for your sake. The captain of that *felucca* wanted a thousand crowns, and he does not look honest. I would not trust you to him.'

'There is another *felucca*, which the postillion hired. It is nearer; we must take it.'

Pelletier nodded, and began to make his way back to where the boats might be seen; Marie began calling for water. The peasant had listened with open mouth to all these exchanges; so one of the vagabonds was a Duchess! But duchesses did not walk the roads barefoot, making for nowhere. He was suspicious, and when he got home that evening would relate it all to his wife and family; meantime, there were the hundred pistoles to be gained. Soon they came to the sea; he put his burden down, and asked for his money. But too much was happening for him even to be heard; the sea was clear of ships, the horizon bare. Both *feluccas* had gone.

'Water,' said Marie faintly. Hortense turned and gathered her up in her arms and paid the peasant, thankful to be rid of him. 'Go, Pelletier,' she said, 'see what you can find. We cannot move from here; my sister is in distress.' After the groom had gone off she wandered about, trying to find a freshet or even a pool which might revive Marie; but there were none. She went back and sat down beside her sister, who by now was a picture of misery, her hair uncoiled and hanging down her back, her feet blistered and raw, her face streaked with tears and dust. Something must happen, thought Hortense; we cannot stay like this. Even an agent of the Colonna might have been welcome.

But it was Pelletier who returned, waving his arms above his head in token of success.

The first *felucca* had been found. They could board at once.

★ ★ ★

They had been rowed out to the boat and climbed up the side, one after the other, Marie somehow managing to make the effort to cling to the ropes; but on arrival on deck, travel-stained as they were, seeming like beggars, they were confronted by a surly and suspicious crew. 'What have you done, killed the Pope?' shouted one. 'Who may you be?'

Pelletier, who was rapidly assuming the habits of a diplomat, had words aside with the captain, money changed hands, and they made ready to set sail. 'I feel sick already,' said Marie, eyes closed against the moving water.

Nobody heeded her; there was the sound of more quarrelling. Pelletier came to them to say that the captain demanded a still larger sum. 'He shall have what he needs,' said Marie faintly, and handed her purse to the groom. 'Only let us be gone.' She retched. 'They shall have more . . . still more . . . when we reach France.'

27

Some nightmares are remembered, and all her life Hortense would never forget the voyage in the *felucca*. No sooner had they boarded than a calm fell for six hours; they had to wait in trepidation, forever fearing that any passer-by might be a spy of the Colonna, even of Mazarin. Night fell, and just before darkness obscured it they could make out a strange vessel, heading towards them; the captain came and roughly told them they must land. 'It is a Turk,' he said. 'You do not want to end up in the slave market, ladies, or the harem.'

They scrambled miserably ashore; even Hortense was beginning to lose her buoyancy of spirit. There was no wood to shelter them tonight; instead, they made do as best they could amongt the rocks, and at some time, seeing that nothing profitable was to be gained by staying, the pirate ship made off. The captain signalled to them by dawn that they could re-embark.

'I would not have been surprised had he made off without us, after taking our money,' remarked Hortense. Marie did not answer except with a moan. Again, they clambered up the ship's sides, and this time left shore. But worse was to come; as though the very gods were angry with them, a great storm-cloud had appeared overhead, and burst to blinding rain as the ship took off; they were tossed like oranges in a crate for six hours, prey to such seasickness that they wished they were dead; suddenly the storm cleared, and they could see green slopes arising above a sandy shore.

'Land here, ladies, for a little,' begged Pelletier, himself gaunt and pale from sickness and hunger. It might be possible, on shore, to find food, though he had the delicacy not to mention it.

'Where are we?' demanded Hortense; Marie still lay prone, her head turned away, her eyes closed.

'We are in Monaco. Rest here till the weather is calmer. Then we will sail on to Marseilles.'

But the *felucca* had too doubtful an identity to use Marseilles harbour; in the end they disembarked at Viotat, and hired horses to take them on to the port. 'I shall never, never,' declared Marie, 'travel by sea again.'

★ ★ ★

There was comfort for them at Marseilles. The Intendant, primed by Monsieur, was waiting for them, and let them hide in his house for several days to recover from the voyage, meantime giving Marie her passport into France. During this time of peace and quiet the sisters had it out with one another; no, Hortense declared, she would not travel with Marie to Paris.

'What? Where will you go? How will I contrive without your company to help me? I must say, you could have told me all this before we set out on this miserable voyage. *Mon Dieu*! When I remember those waves!' Marie leaned her head on her hand, as though to still the echo of the storm still in her ears. Hortense grinned like an urchin.

'You and I have our own ways of contriving, Marie, but they must be separate. We are no longer children. You will do very well with Monsieur's friendship, and if ever you need me, send, and come to stay with me.'

'Stay with you? Name of God! Where?'

'In Savoy. I intend to take up residence there. You may remember that Duke Charles-Emmanuel was an admirer of mine when we were all young. He has not forgotten his chivalry. He has offered me a home for as long as I care to use it.'

181

'Where?'

'In one of his châteaux.'

'You shock me, Hortense! Have you no regard for your reputation?'

'None. It is a cumbersome article, better done without. And you, my dear; you are for Paris?'

'Indeed; where else should I go?'

'I wish you joy, Marie . . . and comfort.' She gazed with pity at the other's averted back. She will not obtain what she wants from Louis, Hortense thought. If not, she may come to Savoy, but I do not think she will; and I rather hope that she does not; whatever she may once have been, she is not entertaining now.

★ ★ ★

The Intendant provided them with transport and they went on by coach to Aix. Here a singular hostess was waiting for them; Madame de Grignan, the young woman who was the daughter of the famous letter-writer, Madame de Sévigné, and thus knew all the news from France. She was a comely, sharp-witted young woman, as might have been expected; but to the pair of castaways she showed nothing but kindness.

'You shall have clean shifts, never fear;

you lost everything in that storm, did you not? I have plenty by me, and can furnish you both.' (What news there would be to write to Mamma, who too often suffered from a lack of excitement over happenings in the provinces!)

They accepted the clean linen gratefully, and stayed a fortnight. By this time, letters, angry ones, had begun to arrive from the Colonna, who had traced them. But there was nothing he could do. Marie was not the only one to be persecuted; Hortense was warned that Polastron, Mazarin's agent, was in the city. It was time to part.

'Farewell, Marie.' Night had fallen, and under cover of it one sister would make for Paris, the other through the mountains towards Chambéry. 'Farewell. We may never meet again.'

'Pray for me, Hortense. Our lives have not fallen out as they should have done. I will remember you in my prayers.' Marie's dark eyes shone with tears. She will never be happy for long, Hortense thought, no matter what happens.

'And I you. Farewell.' The coaches drew apart in the night, one towards the flat western lands, the other to where the incredible mountains reared in their eternal snow. 'Farewell . . . Farewell!'

Marie was to be unlucky, as she had been all her life. First of all the Queen, who was Regent for the time — the King was away making war — refused her entry into French territory; secondly, when she travelled to be near the King at Lyons, he refused to receive her. Marie stood, stunned at the refusal, for a little while; then she lifted her hand to where she might feel the coolness of the Stuart pearls, safe against her throat. He gave me those, at least, she thought; I shall have that, and memory. And for the rest of her life, travelling through one country after another, with no home, no place of rest, Marie Colonna remained as she had been, would always be; even when she was an old, old woman, with all of life gone by. One could remember; and there were the pearls.

28

She lay on a day-bed where the sun flooded
in through the stone-fretted window from the
scorching Savoyard noon. She was barefoot
and wore a loose white shirt like a man's,
linen breeches open at the knee, and her
hair hung like silk as she lay, moving and
stirring in the heat as she leaned over to
feed the nightingales. They were tame and
would take grapes from her. She thrust her
small white hand through the open door
of the cage, a grape between thumb and
forefinger; and they pecked like sparrows.
They did not often sing, but they gave her
pleasure. So did the dogs, lying panting
in the heat. Somewhere, a gentle voice
was reading aloud from Montaigne; it was
Madame Deleschereine, who came daily, and
they would discuss it afterwards and cook
chestnuts in wine. To improve one's mind
while relaxing one's body made life ideal;
she had no troubles here. Charles-Emmanuel
of Savoy had been kindness itself. Hortense
smiled a little: of course she had paid him
in the only way she could; he was not too
happy in his marriage with a strong-minded

wife. He himself was easy-going, generous — look at the way he had sent game, fruit and wine to beguile her last journey to meet poor Marie, who had written to her in distress from Grenoble! But the journey had been wasted; there was nothing she could do for Marie. The other two sisters, naturally, lived their own lives; Marianne and Olympe were bristling with outrage in Paris because she, Hortense, was happy as a country-woman, wearing no shoes, doing what she chose, walking out to shoot when the mood took her, reading or being read to when it did not, entertaining whom she liked at Charles-Emmanuel's expense. Let them lead their stiff narrow lives as they would; she had escaped from all that.

Yes, she was free; at first the sensation had been so heady that she would wake up in the night and think that she had dreamt it all, that, presently, in the dark, Mazarin would turn towards her to take his violent rights. It was different here; Charles-Emmanuel was a gentle lover, and moreover he did not care, was not jealous, if she took pleasure in other men for a little while. Vicard, the Abbé Sanréal, whom he himself had sent to watch over and advise her, had become her lover; he was a writer when he found time, and through the lazy evenings they would discuss the latest news, the latest plays. And Orlier, the castle's Intendant, had fallen at her feet also. It was diverting, and did no one harm.

'Shall I go on?' asked Madame Deleschereine, hesitantly; it was plain that she had not been listened to for some time.

Hortense swung down her linen-clad legs from the day-couch. 'No!' she said, throwing back her hair. 'Let us go out and shoot; it is a glorious day.'

'It is late. The cook will not be able to prepare what we have brought until tomorrow.'

'Then let us content ourselves with wild duck, and keep the quails fresh for next time.' She loved to stop at a country-house or even a monastery to ask the inhabitants to cook what she had shot; once she had taught some monks how to prepare quails in cheese sauce. If the birds were shot cleanly, it was not cruel; what she could not bear was the habit the countrymen had of blinding a quail, caging it, and letting the others draw near because of its cries, when they were trapped and killed. At other times she could be gay over a killing, almost savage; once they had shot a hare and Hortense had split it and plunged her face and arms in the blood. 'It is good for the skin,' she said, and Madame

Deleschereine, who copied her in everything, plunged too, and the pair of them strode through the next village, carrying their guns, bedaubed like primeval savages, sending the children scudding home to their mothers in terror. On that occasion the monks would not let them in.

They did not always dress as men; sometimes she would drive out in one of the Duc's light carriages, handling the reins so boldly that they overturned; but she was not hurt. She had not been hurt, in fact, since that day long ago, which she no longer cared to think of, when she had twisted her knee in the courtyard of an inn and Couberville had worked at it with his strong fingers until it was cured. Where was Couberville now? She hoped he fared well. So many were ruined, or dead; the war was taking its toll; word had lately come that English Madame Henriette, Monsieur's wife, was dead at twenty-six, some thought of poison. 'But everything is not poisoned,' thought Hortense. Madame had been delicate and had had many miscarriages. Perhaps now the Chevalier de Lorraine, Marie's friend, would be permitted again to attend Court. But it will make no difference to Marie, she thought sadly. The King had done with her. Had it been merely for the sake of etiquette, not to offend the Colonna, or perhaps that Louis himself did not want to look on what Marie had become now, remembering what she had once been to him?

★ ★ ★

After the shooting they left two brace of duck with the cook in the kitchen, and Hortense went upstairs and slept the sleep of the healthily tired. She woke, still in darkness, to the growling of the dogs. 'Who is there?' she called out, and sat up to summon Nanon to light a candle; but the dogs subsided, there was silence all around, and she lay down and went back to sleep.

In the morning she saw what it had been. A rat had come in and had eaten the nightingales. There was nothing left of them but a few soft feathers, scattered along the floor.

★ ★ ★

She wept and would not be consoled. If they had been free, not in a cage, they could have escaped. Never again would she keep a caged bird. She lay red-eyed all of the next day, would not be read to, and only when Charles-Emmanuel was announced in the evening put on a bed-gown and had Nanon comb out her hair.

He came in, slight and eager, sympathy on his face for her; he had heard about the nightingales, and had brought her a present to console her — a pair of wriggling spaniel puppies. 'You will be able to train them to the gun, as you are such a marksman,' she heard him say. She went and cast her arms about his neck and then knelt down and played with the puppies, laughing when their milk-teeth bit her playfully. While she did so, Nanon quietly took the nightingales' wooden cage away. Madame had had enough sadness.

★ ★ ★

Intendant d'Orlier was baffled; perhaps bamboozled would better describe his state, for this had been the one he found himself in ever since the arrival at the Château of Chambéry of the mad, beautiful Duchess, who seemed to be so many people at once. At one time he had thought of her as a saint, for she attended Mass constantly, her exquisite face veiled in a black mantilla. He had mentioned the sainthood to the Duc, who laughed heartily, slightly bruising the spirits of d'Orlier; but one day the priest had inveighed against the evils of the theatre and that same evening Madame la Duchesse had been observed seated in her box, surrounded by friends with whom she would eat bread and cheese in the interval. The scales had dropped from M. l'Intendant's eyes and thereafter he had seen Hortense as she was; a child in many ways, learning always; stretching her mind, which had not been previously been given the leisure to improve itself, but now she could talk about anything; prepared to give her incomparable body in return for favours; in other words, a pagan who went to Mass.

He himself had been her lover; he knew the Abbé Saint-Réal had been so; and, of course, Charles-Emmanuel, who doted on her and constantly sent presents, the latest being a pair of engraved pistols and a little Moorish boy in a silver collar. The Moor's name was Mustapha and like everybody else, he adored Hortense on sight. He followed her everywhere, to her box at the theatre or to her gaming-table, where she would wear a mask.

'Why, Madame?' he would ask.

Hortense had laughed. 'So that nobody can see the faces I make when I lose.' They played with her, behind the baffling mask, only aware of her beauty by the matchless arms and hands which dealt and picked up the cards, and, sometimes, the money.

It had been d'Orlier who suggested she should write her memoirs. Secretly, he was worried about Charles-Emmanuel's health; and wondered what would become of beautiful Madame la Duchesse if the Duc were gone. The wife would have her run out of Savoy. So, as the evenings were growing longer and darker, he handed her a quill pen, and said, 'Madame, set down some of your exploits for the world to read!' and she had done so, enjoying the task because it kept her from boredom at not being able to swim naked with Mustapha in the cold lake. After a time the task became the evening's recreation, with Mustapha standing ready to hand fresh sheets of paper, wearing a head-dress Hortense had fashioned for him from muslin and lace. Quickly, the memoirs were finished, and more quickly they sold; nobody was anybody who had not read them. Everyone called at Chambéry, to meet the famous writer. Many editions had of course been printed which contained supplements Hortense had never intended; but that was the way of the world.

* * *

The play on that particular evening had been *Bajazet* by Racine. In her mind ran a certain couplet from it, and when the time came for it to be declaimed on the stage she felt tears start to her eyes, remembering a young, hesitant voice recite the words in a room in the Louvre, amid the smell of paint and oil, and a young man with red-brown eyes gazing at the painter. Then he had kissed her hands. Now he would not even see her.

A rider came galloping in from Turin and was received by the Intendant. He handed him a letter bearing the ducal seal of the House of Savoy. 'It is bad news, sir,' said the man in a low voice while d'Orlier slit the seal. The other looked up.

'The Duke?'

'He is dead. It was sudden. He was not an old man.' The messenger's face bore signs of grief; Charles-Emmanuel had been much beloved, and now a young child must succeed him.

D'Orlier signed himself with the Cross and read the short missive. It was formal, and contained only the information he already had. I must break it to *her*, was his first thought. Later, after he had seen the rider refreshed and his horse rubbed down, he mounted the stairs to where Hortense was to be found. She was painting — it was one of her new pursuits, like cookery and shooting — and turned lustrous eyes on him as he entered.

'Come and look at what I have done,' she said gaily. 'It must be finished today; the flowers will have faded by tomorrow.'

He looked at the bright thing, scrawled and dabbled on canvas; like all the other things she attempted, it was different from anyone else's. Unwillingness rose in him to destroy this brittle joy, this child's paradise. He bowed and said, as the rider had said to him, 'The news is bad. It is from Turin.'

'My Duke?' She laid down her brush, and stood waiting stiffly, like a soldier about to be shot. 'Tell me. He is — ill?'

'He is dead, Madame. His heart failed. As we know, he was not an old man.'

Tears were already running down her face. 'How different it will be here without him! How I shall miss his visits, his thoughtfulness! Do you remember how he used to send fruit and wine when I was going on a journey? And a thousand things . . . '

She turned away from her painting and began to weep. D'Orlier murmured words of comfort, but in his mind was chiefly amazement. She seemed to have not the

194

faintest notion that she would do anything but stay on here. How could she expect the Duke's widow to make that concession?

★ ★ ★

The widow did not. After the funeral ceremonies were over, an order of dismissal came to Chambéry. But as if some besotted god always watched over Hortense, a visitor came at about the same time; Sir Ralph Montagu, an Englishman, close about the King: one time ambassador to the Louvre.

'Why do you not come to England?' he said.

29

She looked at him; she was still recovering from the shock of the Duchess of Savoy's letter. 'England?' she said. 'I know no one there but the King.'

That would be sufficient, he was thinking, for the purposes he and certain others had in mind; this siren with the tumbled blue-black hair might oust the powerful Louise de Kéroualle, whom everyone knew was a spy for France. Hortense Mazarin had no interest in politics; otherwise her king would have used her long ago. Montagu began to question Hortense, always gently.

'The world knows some little of your affairs, madame. This husband, does he still trouble you?'

She spread out her hands in a shrug. 'Mazarin? He will trouble me till I am in my grave, or he in his. He writes and writes. One day it will be a letter promising everything I ask, the next a threat that I must endure penitence in a convent for years before returning to him. I put everything in the fire, and have stayed here — but now — '

He was not to be diverted. 'And — forgive me, madame — the pension Louis promised you, is it paid?'

'Sometimes, and sometimes not. I have had to rely for everything on my dear, dear Charles-Emmanuel, and now he is gone; they are all gone. I shall be an old woman soon.'

'Never, Madame la Duchesse; you are not yet thirty.'

'You know much of me, my lord,' she said innocently.

He thought he had never met a more childlike creature; there would be no hazard from her. Charles would be unable to resist her beauty, her restfulness after the demanding women he had about him. However it was to be achieved, Hortense Mazarin must come to England. 'There is your relative, the Duchess of York,' he added slyly. 'She will be entranced to see you. She has no one to speak Italian with her, and is very lonely.'

'Mary Beatrice,' murmured her aunt. 'I remember Mamma always used to lecture us all regarding the fine marriage my cousin Laura Martinozzi made with the Duke of Modena. And now this daughter is married to the brother of the King of England.'

'Which will place you in high circles at

once; you will not be left to your own resources, as you are here.'

She gave a last glance round the familiar, dear room, stretched out her arms as if in farewell, controlled the tears rising like diamonds in her dark eyes and said obediently, as if a preceptor had spoken, 'I have enjoyed my own resources, as you call it, these past years. But it will be pleasant to be at Court again.' She laughed suddenly. 'The King of England understands French very well, although he used to pretend not to in the days when his mother made him woo La Grande Mademoiselle, who is very plain.'

'As madame says.' Montagu bowed till the curls of his periwig hid his face. He had just brought off a diplomatic triumph; the King of France would not be at all pleased.

* * *

Anyone else would have found it difficult to drum up an escort; Hortense ended with St Réal, Mustapha, a groom, four valets, Nanon, and twenty horsemen. Meantime the widowed Duchess of Savoy had written to Mazarin with leave to arrest his wife within the boundaries of the duchy. But by the time his agent, Polastron, had organised matters accordingly, Hortense had gone; heading for the Swiss frontier, clad once again in man's dress but no periwig, and her hair stuffed under her hat. The riding was rough, uphill and down; incredible heights and impassable gorges reared in their way; they did not deter her, but she avoided the towns; Polastron might catch up with her there. At nights she would find sweet hay in barns and fling herself down on it, weary from the saddle; to watch the stars through the open entry, to watch the dawn rise, became her habit; at last, Savoy of the happy memories was left behind.

She saw the spread blue Swiss lakes, the flung bulk of the Jura separating her from France; it was impossible to enter there, and in the Low Countries King Louis was making war. Well, it must be risked; on passing through Geneva Hortense met a reminder of other days, having worn less well than she had, and sour-faced with it; Sidonie de Courcelles, running away from her husband again. They did not stay long in converse; Sidonie thought Hortense mad, Hortense found Sidonie dull and resentful. If she had had heard the report Sidonie passed round about her afterwards she might have been indignant; she was said to be triumphant by excess of folly. 'Talking of nothing but violins and hunting-parties!' She herself had more serious matters afoot.

The Grignans, with whom Hortense had long ago stayed near Marseilles, were already receiving letters from Madame's mother saying the Duchesse Mazarin was mad. Assuredly the Duc was so, but one was accustomed to that. 'She may even be in England, where as you know there is neither faith, law nor priest! A ballad is being passed about saying she will bring trouble on the King,' concluded Madame de Sévigné.

It looked as though the boot might be on the other foot; she had difficulty in passing the frontiers, made eyes at the officers, got her way, and often wasted a whole day hunting if the weather was right. It was her farewell to Europe; at last, saying goodbye to the escort who had enjoyed the wildest chase across country a woman had ever made, she boarded a packet at Brill. It was stormy; the vessel was driven off course and was lucky to land her at Sole Bay, where by some miracle Montagu was waiting. She sagged into his arms, exhausted. Saint-Réal, Mustapha and the faithful Nanon followed on. 'To London!' they said gaily. 'To London!'

It was near Christmas, and the roads were

frozen and rutted with mud. At last they saw what looked like a bowl of fog.

'The city waits for you,' murmured Montagu obsequiously, but she did not seem to be noted as they rode up a lane between high begrimed houses; this, she was told, was Bedford Street. Then there was a square, where stale vegetables lay about on the ground; this was Covent Garden. 'But it is not a garden,' she protested.

'It used to be. Now it is a market, and in the early morning one may send a servant to buy vegetables fresh from the country, far cheaper than in the shops.'

'That is a comfort.'

She felt homesick suddenly; but for what? Paris was closed to her, Savoy was forbidden. The tall narrow house in the piazza they had taken for her seemed strange and chilly — she had never felt such cold, they must light fires at once — and she flung herself down in a chair and stared up at Montagu, her muddy boots splayed out on the carpet, her hat awry. She pulled off the latter and all her hair came tumbling down.

'You must see that no one knows I am here,' she said, gazing up at him.

★ ★ ★

Montagu did what he could, but it was a hopeless task. Those who came to stare were already at the doorstep, intrigued at the sight of a foreign woman in breeches — one could tell readily that it was no man — who had ridden in after a long, long journey. Who was she? By degrees they guessed that she was of importance; first of all the French Ambassador called, then the Comte de Gramont, eager for scandal. They were in the house together a long time. At last they came out and the waiting crowd held its breath for titbits. They got them.

In the silence the Comte pronounced, as though on a stage, 'She is the most beautiful woman I have ever seen.'

Later an even more important personage, a gentle-faced lady with heavy-lidded dark eyes, called in her gilded coach; it was the Duchess of York herself, Mary of Modena, the beautiful unknown's cousin; and she asked Hortense to a reception. This news upset the Ambassador; he was promptly sent for by Louise de Kéroualle, the King's favourite mistress, to explain his actions, the situation, everything; but words were not enough and everything had gone wrong, and Louise collapsed in hysterics, brown curls and ribbons flying: was she to be superseded after all?

30

'Today I have brought you a pat of good fresh butter. The woman who makes it keeps her cows near the Charter-house, and there are clear green places for them to graze.'

The Seigneur de St Evremond bowed, and presented his gift as if handing diamonds to a queen. Hortense took the package and thanked him by kissing him, regardless of the fact that he was not clean and smelt of ducks' droppings. He was her first friend in England.

'It is too kind of you,' she said. 'Every day you bring a gift, wine, butter, fruit. As you have no more money than I, it is generous.'

'But you, madame, are generous of your company.'

It was true; they would sit for hours and talk of everything under the sun, and he had taught her a great deal she did not know; concerning books, history, music — he sometimes played while her page sang — and other things; he had bought her a whistling bird to add to her ever-increasing menagerie of pets; he had introduced her to people who mattered and who knew him well, despite his odd appearance. He would not wear a wig and his head, covered with a cap for warmth, was fringed with dirty grey wisps of hair. He had a huge wen between his eyes that would have made him seem like some strange animal himself had it not been for the kindness and wisdom in the eyes. He brought what Hortense had never had, the love of a father: he had never tried to become her lover. He would escort her to the play, partner her at cards, fetch her a chair to go to Court as though he had been her servant; and his blood was as old as the Crusades. He had been banished from France by, of all people, Hortense's uncle Cardinal Mazarin; and the Duke of Buckingham had invited him to England. It was natural now that his beautiful protégée should have become familiar with the Buckingham circle, which was opposed to Louise de Kéroualle's influence over the King.

Hortense smiled to herself. She had met Charles, for the first time after many years, at the Duchess of York's reception, had been made known to him and had seen the lazy eyes rake her from head to foot; His Majesty liked what he saw, and by now was a frequent visitor to her in the late evenings, when the others had gone. The house was a better one than the first that had been taken for her in Covent Garden Piazza; through the influence of St Evremond Hortense had rented, at a very low rate, a house in St James's itself. It belonged to the Duke of York, Mary of Modena's husband, the King's younger brother. York himself she had not been able to subdue.

'James prefers ugly women,' the King had said once, when she mentioned her lack of success with the Duke. 'It is a compliment to your beauty, *ma belle*, that he ignores you. Even his wife does not rouse fire in him. I never knew such a fellow.'

'I can remember the days when Your Majesty paid court to an ugly woman.'

'More than one, ferreted out by my mother,' grimaced the King. 'There was a Dutch wench, and then . . . but I made an offer for myself whose results would have been pleasing had it been permitted.' The melancholy eyes surveyed her. She smiled sadly.

'Do you know that they never told me, till after I was married to Mazarin, that you had made an offer for me when I was only twelve years old? Then later, when you were restored to your throne, my uncle had the impertinence to write again and say that the offer might be reconsidered. I do not blame

Your Majesty's advisers for replying that a bride who had been refused during the days of penury could hardly be accepted in the days of wealth.'

'It was not wealth, only a crown. How I wish we had been left to arrange matters for ourselves!' They stared at one another, each thinking how different their lives would have been if they had been allowed to marry in youth: enough money for Charles out of the Mazarin inheritance, and no mad husband to torment Hortense and destroy a collection of masterpieces. 'No, you would have housed the statues and paintings carefully, for your own father was a great connoisseur, was he not?' she said.

'Ay, and Cromwell sold many of his finest paintings abroad.' The King's tone was bitter; she recalled that he liked to be distracted, and asked if he would like some music, or a game of cards. Charles shook his head, its black curled periwig setting off his harsh dark features. 'I like to sit here and talk with you. Tell me how St Evremond fares. When they objected to my making him an allowance I told them I had put him in charge of the ducks in St James's Park.'

'He would like that. He keeps ducks and all kinds of other birds and animals in his lodging, and the stink is unbearable. He

206

relieves himself as they do, in the rooms. I love him dearly, but after he has been here I get Nanon to burn a shovelful of lavender before Your Majesty's visits.'

'You are fastidious; it is one of the things I like in you.' His glance indicated that there were others; she surmised that, as he sometimes did, he would like to make love with her on the bed. She had come to England prepared for this, and had been amused at how soon it had happened. Louise Portsmouth could continue in her hysterics. Hortense liked the King; she had begun to like life at the Court of St James's, and best of all she liked droll St Evremond, who kept her up to scratch with the world's gossip. But they all knew — except the King of France and Louise herself — that Hortense was no whit interested in politics, and had no ambitions to direct the fortunes of a country, hold the strings of diplomacy in her hands; she would rather hold the reins of a good horse. Charles knew this, and knew that she knew, and the little game continued to the amusement of all of them.

★ ★ ★

Charles would not be ungallant enough to reveal bedroom secrets, but on one memorable occasion he talked to Hortense of Louise de Kéroualle. 'The wretch troubles herself profoundly about you,' he told her. 'The ministers of His Most Christian Majesty Louis XIV are in a continual ferment, and keep her so, lest she lose her hold on my person and, accordingly, allow to diminish the supposed interests of France in this land.' He smiled, moving one shapely hand to warm it at Hortense's fire. 'The world knows, and you know also, how I came to meet with Louise. It was on the last occasion my beloved sister, Minette, Madame d'Orléans, visited me before her death. We made merry together and before we parted, she brought out her jewel-case and asked me to choose a jewel as a keepsake; I think we both knew that we would not meet again. I, with my roving eye, had remarked the little maid who brought the jewels, and I asked my sister for her. She refused; she had promised the girl's mother to bring her back safe to France. So Louise went, and soon came the news of my sister's death.' He fell silent for moments, placing his hand over his eyes. 'When I could think clearly again,' he said, 'I asked Louis to send me Louise de Kéroualle. It seemed to me that I had snatched a life from a death. She gave me something for which to live. I am aware that she is greedy, dabbles in politics, convinces Louis — although not myself — that she maintains the French alliance my dear Minette had come here to ratify. But all this means nothing to me when I see her pink cheeks and blue ribbons. I lost one thing and gained another; Fubbs, I call her. You and she must meet; the fanning of the ridiculous enmity must end. She can chatter French with you, Hortense; that will divert her. And you are too good-natured to let this talk of mine arouse in you the jealousy that has made poor Fubbs take one crying fit after another, since you came. You are, you see — ' the hand reached out to caress Hortense's cheek — 'so very beautiful.'

'I will meet her gladly.'

'Knowing that I love her?'

'Love is a thing that has passed me by. I have been loved by many, and have had many friends. But to love? I do not know what it means; oh, yes, I can give and take pleasure in bed. My husband Mazarin has written to me lately again about two years' penance in a convent before he will see me again. I have lived my life.'

'You have half your life to come, and may it be happy.'

'Not so. I found grey hairs the other day. I will not dye them. We must all grow old.' She shifted restlessly. 'I must tell Your

Majesty that the other day, the Ambassador, de Ruvigny, and Courtin who will shortly succeed him, visited me. Their object will make you laugh.'

'Then by all means let me hear it.' Charles let his heavy eyelids droop over his eyes, and continued playing with Hortense's little dog, as he had done since he came in. 'It is more diverting here than when we used to meet in my sister-in-law's apartments,' he said. 'You hold your own Court here; you have no need of St James's.'

'And, thanks to your pension, no need of France.'

'What did they try to make you do?'

'Work for them, under the threat that if my husband Mazarin did not restore my great jewels and my allowance, I would oust the Duchess of Portsmouth — '

'Fubbs.'

' — that I should oust Fubbs and turn Your Majesty away from the contemplation of the great benefices you win by accomodating France and her King.'

'You let them go away believing that?'

'I agree to everything. I have found it is the best way to be left in peace, if one pleases everybody.'

'You please me,' he said. He leaned over her and caressed her neck below the ear.

Mon Dieu, this is as far as St Evremond goes, she thought, but always at cards. Last time she had said to him, 'Is it Gabrielle d'Estrées you are courting?' Now, she might be any woman . . .

Later, in bed, he said to her, 'Hortense, you must not die without having loved. You are the perfect mistress, the divine companion. But you must learn to love till it grips the guts and stops the heart. Without that, you have not lived.'

'Shall I love Your Majesty?' It would not be hard, she thought; his notable face, with the deep lines carved from nose to mouth, lay by her, and the incomparable Stuart hand lay on her breast. At her words he smiled. 'No, it is too late,' he said. 'But I pray — and I think of God at times, Hortense — that you may not leave this life without first having known everything it can give.'

She saw him go, as dawn came up on the river. She knew he would return and that Fubbs, Nell, other mistresses, of which there were many, would make no difference to his relations with her unless she offended him. And that she would not willingly do. It was not only the pension.

31

It was impossible, in fact, to avoid meeting Fubbs, for the Court moved and mingled constantly. At Windsor with its great round tower Hortense stared at the ageing Prince Rupert's doughty collection of historic armour, grouped and hanging on the walls; at Newmarket she heard the thundering of hooves and the excited bets of my lords and ladies as to who should carry off the Plate; and, once, watched a handsome young man win it, his cheeks flushed and his dark curls flying as he bowed before his father, the King, and bore away the heavy trophy. Everyone clapped and cheered except the Duke of York, who looked sour; the enmity between himself and his nephew Monmouth was such that soon one of them would have to go abroad.

Hortense made friends in her ready way and could not afterwards recall her first meeting with Louise de Kéroualle. Certainly there was a party given in which everybody had to imitate a horse and rider, much wine was drunk and she and Louise emerged, hand in hand and screaming with laughter, from a cupboard; but the memory of that had grown dim. There was a more sober meeting on the square of turf at Tunbridge Wells, where the men played bowls or croquet in the evenings while during the day it was surrounded with booths in which pretty girls, in caps and prints and white cotton stockings, sold musk and lavender, strawberries, butter, anything one wanted.

Yes, it had been there, on the summer grass. Hortense remembered the small plump figure, the babyish face with its round pink cheeks enhanced by rouge, the blue eyes of which one was marred ever so slightly by a cast, so that Nell Gwynn mocked at Squintabella. Louise was elegant; she wore a blue gown with a scarf of fine lawn cast over her head and shoulders so that the sun would not burn her skin. She and Hortense were courteous to one another, and talked for some moments about acquaintances in France. Both women were aware that all eyes were upon them, and it was only afterwards that one remembered the mock wedding at a country-house, where Louise had been bedded and a stocking flung when the King climbed in with her, as though they had been bride and groom.

The Queen?

The Queen came to Tunbridge Wells also;

sometimes players were brought down for her to watch. Hortense had been formally presented to her by the Duchess of York and Catherine had been kindly, and they had made talk; but the Queen seldom joined the revels, making her own life at St James's and at Somerset House, where she often lived alone. She had far more character than Louis' queen, and the long hazel eyes saw most things; but years ago Catherine of Braganza had learned silence. There was only one old story about an outburst of resentment because Barbara Castlemaine, the King's first mistress who was now Duchess of Cleveland, had been put on the bride's list of ladies of the bedchamber. The King never went to Barbara now. Their son Grafton, and their daughter the Countess of Sussex, a little nervous creature, were often at Court. Poor little Sussex had been married while very young to a brute, and avoided him whenever possible. At an early stage Hortense found that she was adored.

'Madame Mazarin, how lovely you are. I love you, I swear it. Do you love me? I should like to have a little portrait of you, to kiss when you are not there.'

Hortense was too good-natured to shake off this child who clung to her for company. Soon it became a matter of seeing young Lady

Sussex each day, having her in the house each night, playing cards and — this was what eventually caused the trouble — fencing, for Hortense had taken instruction in France and had mentioned it, and nothing would do but that the little creature be instructed in it too. 'Let us wear shirts and breeches, and practise outside under the trees!' the child begged.

'Wait till you are recovered from your confinement.' The Countess had just borne a child to her husband, and Hortense had helped to nurse her through the recovery, turning liking to adoration; after that, everything she did must be copied. So it had come to the shirts and breeches. Hortense grimaced when putting hers on; she had gained weight in London, though everyone said it became her, especially . . . especially the Prince of Monaco.

'He would become my lover,' Hortense thought, flexing her weapon. But she had told St Evremond and he had been horrified. 'You cannot cuckold the King,' he said. All the same it would be pleasant to have that young, muscular body close to hers, that young mouth pressed against her open one, a night with youth . . . He had stood by her the other day to watch the Lord Mayor's show, and they had all been clad in furs against the cold of November; there had been fireworks and squibs, and one had hit poor little Sussex in the eye, nearly blinding her. My lord of Sussex had thundered about the incident and had tried to take his wife back home; but here they were, going out in dressing-gowns into St James's Park, peeling them off, revealing the tight breeches and loose white shirts, and saluting, then the clangour of weapons sounded to the cheers of the crowd who had gathered. Crowds would always gather to see Hortense.

Afterwards an unpleasant thing happened. Sussex himself came for his wife, and took her away, despite her protests. Later they heard that he was raping her nightly, and that she had fallen ill. The doctors advised hunting and coursing, but poor Lady Sussex had little time for either; in a very short time she was pregnant again. 'She keeps your portrait in her room and covers it with kisses,' said a courtier to Hortense. The latter was sorry; but was not that the way husbands behaved? Mazarin would have acted in exactly the same way.

32

On a certain morning St Evremond approached Hortense's doorstep as Monaco was being shown out, unshaven. He bowed punctiliously, making no scene in the street; once inside he was told Madame la Duchesse was in her bath. When she came to him, warm, fragrant, and contented, he flayed her. Her dark eyes opened wide; she had never seen, or imagined, St Evremond angry.

'Are you determined to ruin yourself?' he asked her.

She shrugged. 'To take a lover for the night is not ruin, if one chooses carefully.' She shot a teasing glance up at him. Although he had said many times that he could not expect her to love him physically, she knew very well that had he been a younger man, and presentably handsome, he would have been in the lists. As it was, the dismay and reproach on his face almost made her laugh. 'Cheer yourself, Knight of the Doleful Countenance,' she murmured; it was the name she used to him in letters.

'It is for you I am anxious. Your French pension has been cut off because the King there knows you have not the interests of France at heart — '

'I have nobody's interests at heart, except my own.'

' — and do you suppose that when the King here learns of this, as he will, he will laugh at it?'

'He laughed at great Barbara Cleveland, when John Churchill had to escape out of her window without his breeches, when the King came in.'

'That was when the King had long done with the Duchess of Cleveland, except in friendship and a kind of pity. You are still his mistress; you should be no other man's.'

★ ★ ★

It did not seem as if her escapade had made any difference; the Prince of Monaco continued to spend delightful nights with her, and the King, as was his wont, strolled in in the evening now and again, when he had already visited Louise Portsmouth and the card-playing was finished. He seemed affable, but when the time came for Hortense's pension to be paid, it was not.

★ ★ ★

She was in despair; how was she to live? She clawed her hair, pulling at the silken locks till her scalp hurt; St Evremond had been right, of course. Where was she to go now? She had no home but England; everywhere else, Mazarin's arrest awaited her. When St Evremond came in she wept.

'How am I to go on?' she wailed. 'Does the King desire that I should go abroad again? I have hardly the fare, and no protector.'

St Evremond did as he often did, and gave her a kiss on the tip of the ear. 'Wait for a little while,' he whispered. 'It will come right. But — no more night adventures! Keep yourself as chaste as Diana.'

To Monaco's credit, he did not force her to continue their affair and, also, he contributed money to a fund St Evremond set up for her. Thus she was able to continue for a little while in her usual state; and there was no open quarrel with the King. When the next quarter-day came round, her pension was paid; but it was halved. Better than nothing, by far; and a lesson.

* * *

She had been writing her memoirs, and though they tended to be one-sided, presenting Hortense always as the persecuted innocent, they were diverting, and would sell. She heard news of their popularity in France, whence Louis XIV's ambassador had lately written to his King, 'You must get her back *at all costs*. She is dangerous to France because of her beauty and her resentment towards Your Majesty.' Truth to tell Hortense resented no one, not even Mazarin; if she and Louis had confronted one another, she would have been as affable as in the old days when he was in love with Marie.

33

The Countess of Sussex had obtained permission from her father to leave her brutal husband, on condition that she kept open house for him to visit his mistresses. Despite the French Ambassador's efforts to give a party at which everybody had to imitate a horse, Louise and Hortense were still on wary terms; perhaps more could not be expected. Charles still visited Louise in the afternoons, Hortense in the evenings; and this was enough to send the echo of wailing across the Channel to Paris, where Louis XIV, amused, began to refer to Louise Portsmouth as the Dolorous Signora.

Hortense, after her experience with the pension, was trying to live on less. Instead of going to the shops for stuffs for her gowns, she went down to the docks, buying them as they came off the ships. The lascars stared at the beautiful woman in the hooded cloak whose hands were whiter than a shopkeeper's, yet she bargained like one; she would return home in her coach with satin, velvet, brocade and lawn, got at low prices, rolled on the seat opposite, and Nanon's shrewd eye inspecting everything.

Nevertheless she did not save, because as soon as she had money she spent it needlessly. One evening she won six thousand crowns from a Portuguese visitor, and instead of hoarding it fitted out all her footmen in gold livery. Her extravagance was talked about, and ballad-sheets were being sold about her in the streets; naturally, everyone thought the King had paid for the liveries.

Both bad and good news came out of France. Marie-Charlotte, her eldest daughter, whose features she had almost forgotten, ran away from her convent to marry the Duc de Richelieu, by whom she was pregnant. It might have been worse; but the good news followed, which was that her brother Philippe was to visit London.

'I cannot count the years since we met,' said Hortense joyfully to St Evremond. 'Will he have changed, do you think?'

'He will at any rate be amazed that *you* have not.' The old man gazed at her dark, perennial beauty; her figure had grown a little fuller, but it suited her and was the fashion of the day. They said Louise Portsmouth was growing frantic for some means of putting on flesh. But when Philippe arrived, and was made known to the courtiers, the first thing he did was to make improper advances to Louise; this was foolish, as she was invariably correct and faithfulness to the King was her trump card. Philippe returned to his sister with a rueful grin on his face, which had grown hard and grey.

'I have been given my marching orders, and told to leave England,' he said.

'And serve you right. I am sorry the visit has been so short. When will we meet again, my Philippe?'

'The sooner the better. I have always loved you.'

She saw him go with anguish; he had brought back brief memories of Paris, the Louvre, old friends, the leaves falling into the Seine. In her bones she felt they would never meet again.

34

It was hard to think of the King as growing old; but events wearied and aged him. There had been the Popish Plot, when Titus Oates had forced him, the merciful, to execute innocent Catholics and send his brother abroad. He came to Hortense for comfort, perhaps because, as a Catholic, she might also be persecuted: a Popish whore and French agent, Oates called her. Yet she showed no fear, as Louise Portsmouth was doing, crouching in her house planning flight. By day Hortense would walk with St Evremond in the gardens of Boughton, which belonged to their old friend Sir Ralph Montagu; by night, at home, there were cards and conversation as usual, and it was said her house was not attacked because she had Huguenot servants. Also, Monmouth the Protestant hero was her friend. One night the King came and stayed after the others had left.

'Cheer me, Hortense,' he said. 'Already you do so by looking as beautiful as I have ever seen you. The new gown becomes you well.' He had paid for a black and gold flowered satin gown for her, trimmed with gold lace, with a matching cloak.

'But beauty alone does not cheer you tonight.' She understood him and there was nothing of the coquette in her tone; it was one of the reasons why he was fond of her; she listened and understood.

'You know that your Mazarin wrote to tell me your I.O.U.'s were valueless,' he told her.

'That was not gallant of him. I will tell you a story about my page, Déry,' she said. 'He has an angelic singing voice as you know. Now he talks of having himself castrated to keep it.'

'He will regret what he has lost far more than what he gains. Do not permit him to do anything so barbarous.' The King shifted his long body in the chair. 'Divert me, Hortense. They say you can dance the tarantella. Dance it for me, this night.'

'But there is no music.' St Evremond, who generally played for them, was not present.

'Then *I* will play,' said Charles Stuart. Her brows flew up in surprise, and he laughed. 'You do not think a King can have any talents but those of love and war? Try me. When I was a child my father had me taught to play both the lute and the guitar.' He stretched out an idle hand, its cuff-lace falling back, to receive the instrument from her. She was laughing.

'If we have both forgotten our talent, it will be a sorry show.'

'But nobody will know of it except ourselves.' He struck a chord. She began the half-remembered figures, the twisting and weaving of the limbs, making the gaudy skirts flow; presently her body became a miracle of fluid rhythmic grace, her hands clapping in the absence of castanets, urging on the hesitant music he made, pleasuring him so that he became adept. When it was over he kissed her. 'We can make our living together on the streets, if need be,' he said. 'I am not sure that I would not dispense with all I have to do so, at this moment.'

'Now you are growing melancholy again. Let us go and feed the birds and dogs; they always wait for your coming.'

She watched him caress the little dogs, whom he loved; and as always felt admiration for him, for his tolerance, his humour, his patience. She knew, as everyone did, that he had not deserted his Catholic Queen in this crisis but on the contrary, had sent for her to stay by him at Whitehall. 'They say he forgets friends, but he does not,' she thought, and remembered the ballad-sheet about them both that had been brought to her notice a little while ago; it did not disturb her either.

226

Away with fulsome Mazarine,
And give us back our Charles again.

But she would keep him from nobody; neither his people, his son, his brother, nor Louise Portsmouth.

35

She had remained faithful to Charles since the Monaco incident, not entirely for financial reasons; she was fond of him, and he had enough to bear in these years; shortly after the quelling of the Popish Plot, Monmouth, the beautiful and favoured, had to be banished the Court, which made the King sad. The truth was, if anyone were to admit it, that Monmouth considered himself the legitimate heir to the throne and that his father, in the years before the Restoration, had been married in secret to his mother, Lucy Walter. There were those who spoke up for and against it; foremost among Monmouth's supporters was Shaftesbury, the Protestant champion; again Louise Portsmouth was afraid, then tried to ally herself with the Green Ribbon Boys, as Shaftesbury's supporters were known; but they would have none of her.

Hortense allied herself with nobody, and went on living her own life as she chose. She loved to gallop in the early morning over the turf on Newmarket downs, regretting Monmouth's handsome presence no more seen; but instead she had a host of followers, almost all of whom had tried to become her lovers without success; there was Arran, Derwentwater, Devonshire and many others, bewigged and gallant. They wheeled about and urged their horses to the long gallop which later in the day would see the ribbon cut and the Plate given; how soon would Monmouth be free to win it again? It was his uncle's jealousy, they whispered, more than Shaftesbury's plotting, which had made it needful for him to retire from Court for the time being.

'Who are those riders?' asked Hortense, slowing her mare to a canter. They made a dark patch against the green of the downs and the light morning sky. Her party made towards them with a hollaing and cheering, for all who met on the King's ride were friends; as they grew nearer, Hortense made out one rider in particular, tall and easy in the saddle. He wore a grey riding-cloak and his hat bore no plume. Blue eyes, shrewd and appraising, met her own; she felt herself blushing, and weakness rise. Who was he? She had never, to her certain knowledge, met him before. She knew, as though they had told her in so many words, that she would remember this instant, this meeting, all her life.

He slid from the saddle and came to kiss her hand, the only woman as she was among a party of men. 'Baron de Banier,' she heard Arran's voice inform her softly. 'He is from Sweden, but will speak French with you.'

The Baron's blunt features were amiable, but set; he did not try to pay compliments. How could she make him speak? The blue eyes were set off by thick brows, of a darker colour than his hair which, now the hat was swept off for courtesy, revealed itself as reddish gold. He was very tall, taller than any of these Englishmen or than anyone she had encountered in France.

'I shall be pleased to welcome you to my house, Baron,' she heard her voice say; to her amazement, it sounded uncertain as a child's. Who was this man that he should set her trembling? She recalled the words of old St Evremond. 'You were made to be loved, not to love.' It was absurd to think that she had permitted herself to fall in love with a foreign stranger she might never see again, if he chose not to visit her.

★ ★ ★

But he called. There was company, as always, and she was afraid that he would go away, wearied of the talk in a tongue that was not his own. He played cards, competently, laughing with the rest when Hortense as usual cheated in the Italian manner. He drank wine with them all in silence, and waited and waited; at last, they were alone.

They did not speak. She saw his tall muscular figure — he must have fought in many wars, but thank God it had not scarred his face — stand in her room, with its carefully chosen furnishing, as though he had been the only object in it; if she must choose, she would throw away the marbles, the velvets and chairs and bird-cages, and keep him, him only. *You were born to be loved.* Could he love her? For she loved him, she knew; it had never happened to her before, and she was a woman of thirty-seven whose bones had turned to water.

She held out her hands, her white hands so many men had kissed; how she wished she could have come to him virgin, as she had been for Mazarin all those years ago! They did not speak; he had taken her hands and held them against his cheek, and she could feel its rough manly surface. Then she was in his arms; the buttons of his doublet chafed her cheek, and she would have a little red patch tomorrow, but it did not matter; nothing mattered but that this should have come to her at last. If the King stopped her allowance again, she thought suddenly, she would walk with Baron de Banier a beggar through the streets.

'You, too?' he said wonderingly. 'I am no one, but you, the most beautiful of women . . .'

'I am no one either,' she told him. 'All these years I have been no one, only myself, but now . . .'

They guided one another towards the bed. She did not remember his undressing her, only waking, naked, at some time in the night, to find his arms still hard about her, and to recall their love.

36

Olympe de Soissons, Hortense's sister, was not invited to Versailles nowadays; in fact she had been requested to leave France, and lived meantime in the Low Countries. She had been deeply involved in the poisoning scandal which had lately entrapped hundreds from high to low in France, including the King's mistress, Madame de Montespan.

Olympe's son Philippe was a young man now, and anxious to see the world. To lure him away from France, where she knew he would not be in favour, his mother wrote to her sister Hortense in London asking for her hospitality for Philippe, who should be dear to her because he had been called after their brother, Philippe de Nevers. Hortense received the letter and was in fact most unwilling to have Philippe as a guest in her house at such a time; it could not have been more ill chosen, and she lived for no one but de Banier. However she could not refuse Olympe, and wrote to say that her son would be welcome.

Philippe arrived finely turned out, already in debt to his tailor. He was a susceptible young man and, on kissing his beautiful aunt's hand, fell promptly in love with her. He followed her everywhere, gazing into her face in a manner she found embarrassing; she had changed so greatly with de Banier's love that she had less heedless confidence than formerly. Moreover she set her mind less on entertaining Philippe than she should have done; she asked St Evremond to introduce him at Court, and saw him kiss the King's hand, and Charles quip in the way he had about the times he himself recalled Olympe at the Louvre. 'You have a look of her,' he added, dismissing the young man; in fact Philippe was not taking, having eyes with the whites surrounding them like a nervous horse. He would pick quarrels easily.

Feeling as he did about Hortense, it was not long before he discovered that of all her little circle she best loved de Banier, and that drove him to distracted anger. What right had this Swedish nobody to take up his glorious aunt's time, mind, body? He must be got rid of; so ran Philippe's way of thinking, almost at once. He knew what must be done; he proceeded to do it.

He waited till all of Hortense's guests except de Banier had taken their night's leave, then made pretence to go to his own room; but halfway along the passage he stopped, concealing himself behind a curtain. He saw Hortense come up and go to her room alone, and Nanon enter to undress her, and then come out. He had not heard the Baron leave. He waited a little longer, then had his reward. The big figure of the Swede came into view at the end of the passage, and made as if to turn into Hortense's room. Philippe rushed forward, and cast his gauntlet in the other's face:

'You insult my family. I will avenge it. Name your seconds, and I will name mine.' He knew two young hotbloods who would serve; there were plenty about Court.

De Banier had reeled back against the blow from the glove; now he picked it up and held it out to the offender. 'You are a foolish boy,' he said quietly. 'I do not cross swords with children.'

'By God, if you will have it so I will run you through now!' Philippe drew out his sword with a hissing sound; they still spoke in whispers. 'I will have you know I have killed my man on three occasions,' he said, which was a lie; but once he had in fact won in such an encounter, and this time his blood was up; he could not but win.

The door opened and Hortense stood there, in her night-gown; it was of transparent stuff and showed the candle-light through from the room behind. 'What is the matter?' she said. 'Philippe, why are you not in bed? You went up an hour ago.'

She turned to de Banier and laid a hand on his arm. Philippe began to rave. 'You will ask him, no doubt, why he is not in bed also — and with yourself! It is a disgrace to the family.' Philippe heard his own voice a trifle high-pitched, like a young rooster crowing on the heap. De Banier brushed Hortense's hand gently away and took a step forward.

'Young man, you will collect such things as you need and find yourself room at an inn. You have trespassed on this lady's hospitality long enough and your presence is objectionable.' The voice was still quiet; de Banier seldom lost his temper. On Philippe's refusing to move, he took the boy by the collar, propelled him to the stairs, and escorted him down and out of the house. On the steps, he flung him money.

'That will buy you a night's lodging,' he said, and went in, shutting the door behind him. Later he returned to Hortense.

'I have taken the precaution of telling your servants not to admit him if he tries to enter,' he said. 'Are you angry? Do you wish me to go also?'

'You know very well I would have you stay always.' She was trembling; Philippe in his rage had reminded her of Mazarin. She turned her head and buried her face in de Banier's coat; he guided her into their room and bed, as though she had been blind.

37

De Soissons' seconds were young hotbloods who could be found anywhere; they ran de Banier to earth in a coffee-house the Swedish residents in London frequented. Shoving their way through the crowd to where he was, they delivered Philippe's challenge, standing back afterwards with hands on hips in an attitude of insult. They neither knew nor cared what the dispute was about; they were good for witnessing a fight, that was all.

'Name your seconds.' He had not done so; he was reluctant to consider further what he considered to be a schoolboy's rudeness; it would be best ignored. But by now heads in the room had begun to turn and men laid down their news-sheets and their cups of coffee and the long pipes they smoked; everyone was waiting for de Banier's reply, and he would not make a fool of himself by publicly refusing the challenge. He turned to the man on his left and the man on his right, both of whom he knew; the matter was settled, though afterwards they said to him, 'You should not get embroiled; they say that young devil de Soissons is adept with swords.'

'Then we will make it pistols.'

But swords it was, in the grey early morning of Lincoln's Inn Fields. A few watchers had come, for the news had spread through town; a surgeon waited, wrapped in his cloak against the cold before the sun rose. The duellists removed their coats and edged into position, their breeches and white shirts sadly reminiscent of Hortense and little Sussex, when they had fought thus for a jest. But this was no jest; Philippe de Soissons laid about him as if the very devil was behind him, urging him on. The other was quieter, defending himself ably enough; but it was only defence, not attack, and the watchers could see that he had no heart to wound the boy who had set his heart on killing him. At last Philippe got under de Banier's guard; at last the great thrust of his blade went through the other's body, causing the blood to spurt red even before de Banier fell to the ground. The surgeon hastened with great strides to him, but it was too late; his heart's blood was already soaking into the earth.

★ ★ ★

It was St Evremond who brought the news to Hortense. She had risen late, for de Banier had visited her the previous night and had been as tender with her as though they said farewell. She thought of him, stifling a yawn as she smiled at the grotesque old man. He has brought no gift today, she thought; his hands hung empty.

'Dear Knight of the Doleful Countenance, what ails you?' She came and kissed his cheek; she never made him feel that he was too ugly to touch. Now, his ugliness was forgotten; he had nothing in his mind but grief.

'Much ails me, my dearest one; the news is bad.'

'The King?' Oddly enough her first thought was for Charles; then for Mazarin; he had been pestering her with letters lately, with the usual swing of the pendulum from desire to be with her again to insistence that she should enter a convent and do penance for two years.

'Not the King.' He had shaken his head. 'Someone you love much more. You must be brave, *chérie*; I did not want you to hear it from some idle informant. It is — '

'De Banier. It can be no one else. Is he — ?'

'He is dead. Your nephew killed him in

a duel. He died bravely. That you should know.'

He had seen her turn white as paper, and raise her hand to her breast. 'Philippe,' she repeated. 'I shall never see Philippe again. Tell him not to come here.'

'He is already on the Channel; they smuggled him out, in spite of the Swedish ambassador. He will not come back to England now; you will have peace from him.'

'Peace,' she repeated. As she stood there the tears began to roll down her face, without any grimacing or sobbing; she stood there, while they splashed on her morning-gown; he had to take her and guide her to a seat. She sat there like a doll, obedient, silent, while the tears still came.

'I will send for your maid,' he said comfortingly. 'You should see no one today. Go to bed, and take a little laudanum. Time will heal your grief. Time . . . '

'Time lasts forever,' she said strangely. 'I shall never — never — forget.' She had not looked at him again; he might not be in the room. Familiar with her house as he was, he went to the inner door and sent for Nanon, told her what had happened, what was needed, and returned. Hortense still sat where she had been, weeping silently.

Nanon came. 'Come, my darling.' How many years had they been together now? 'There is a hot brick in your bed, and you will go and lie down in it, and take a little *tisane*, then you will sleep. No one shall come to you. I myself will guard the door.' The woman's full, honest face was stained with tears, for although she had had no great acquaintance with de Banier she knew her mistress loved him.

★ ★ ★

Black; everywhere in the house was hung with black, by her orders. When she had come to herself she had fallen into a frenzy of ordering, supervising the hangings, then falling back on her bed again like a dead woman. On awaking she would stare at the black curtains, reminded at once of what had happened instead of, as might otherwise have been, thinking for moments that all was as usual, till she remembered; and then the sudden remembrance would be like a sword in her heart.

Black everywhere; no guests. Nanon and the men-servants were loyal and had admitted no one. She had not thought to ask where they were burying de Banier, or if they would take his body back to Sweden. A body did

242

not matter by itself. He had gone from her; she had no way of reaching him. She had tried, from her scattered and neglected remembrance of the Catholic prayers for the dead, to pray. *Eternal rest grant unto them, O Lord, and let perpetual light shine on them; may they rest in peace.* But he had been active and at one with the world, loving worldly things as she did. He would be lost now, in the infinite spaces. *Out of the depths have I cried to Thee, O Lord.* She had forgotten the rest. The depths. She was in them now. Nothing that had ever happened to her in all her life had caused her such grief. Her life? What was that worth now, when yesterday it had been so precious? Not yesterday . . . four days now. Four days, and all the years of her life to be lived till they met again. How did one pass such time? Perhaps she would join Marie in her Spanish convent. But even there, how could one forget?

★ ★ ★

'It is the King, Madame.'

'I will see no one.' She was lying in bed, face thrust in the pillow, hair loose and tangled against the linen sheets. Nanon stroked it gently; she had not been permitted to comb it or do anything for her mistress since the death. 'You cannot refuse the King, madame,' she was saying gently. From the door a deep voice echoed. 'No, indeed. You cannot refuse the King who comes to comfort you.' He laid his hand on the shoulder of Mustapha, who had never left his post outside the door night and day: and came in.

The servant went out and he was left alone with her. She did not move and he went to the bed and lifted her up bodily in his arms and sat with her against his knees, her head on his shoulder. A smell of stale sweat came to his nostrils; he had never known that from her before; her face was bloated with weeping and her hair felted so that no comb would go through. He caressed her as he knew so well how to do, then fell to stroking the matted hair and kissing her as though she were a child.

'My poor girl,' he said. 'Listen to me and you will know why I forced my way into your house; an ungentlemanly thing to do.' The wry smile came; against her scalp she felt the muscles of his face move. The apathy she had been in began to leave her and she moved her own head so that she could see him; he raised a hand, turning her cheek to lie against his own.

'You did not even wonder,' he told her,

'why I was not angry with you for this affair, as I was when you gave yourself to Monaco? But I knew you did not love Monaco and that you were behaving like a little *cocotte*. This time, it was different. Old St Evremond has always said that you were made to be loved, not to love. But unless one loves, Hortense, one has not lived. You have lived life to the full now; you have known love and grief. You can be like a goddess now, full of wisdom.'

'You are wise,' she said suddenly, her voice hoarse as though she had forgotten how to speak. 'Have *you* loved?' It did not seem an impertinence at this moment to ask him, the King of England, such a thing. Charles paused in his stroking of her hair, smiled, and said 'As you know, I have been — fond of — many women; yourself, Louise, poor Nell, Moll Davis, Barbara in her day — I am still fond of Barbara — and my sister Minette; my wife; and long ago the mother of my son, Lucy Walter.'

She noticed that he spoke of Lucy as though she were the only woman who had borne him a child. 'I think,' he said, speaking more to himself than to her, 'that there have been two great loves in my life; my father and my son. That is odd, is it not, in a man who womanises as I do? But when they cut off my father's head I learned what grief was, and humiliation. And my son, whom I cannot see any more now, is constantly in my thoughts. I do not know what will become of Monmouth, nor can I alter his fate.'

He stopped speaking and turned to her. 'Lacking you,' he said, 'my Court is dull, worthy, all the things a Court should never be. Will you not let Nanon cut off these tufts of hair that will never admit a comb, dress the rest of it and yourself and come, even to play a game of cards? If you win, it will cheer you a little; if you lose, it will make you angry, and that is better than lying alone with your face to the wall. My dearest girl, if all the world did so, what would become of us?'

She nodded at last, like a child who has agreed to take medicine. 'For you,' she said, 'I will come.' It was better than the convent. She knew now that she could never have endured that.

38

St Evremond had haunted the street daily by the hour, almost weeping; having handed in the many comforting letters he wrote to Hortense he hoped for a reply, but none came. He thought of all their years of friendship together, the way he had even made scented cushions for her to sit on when she visited his rooms, because she found the smell his ducks' droppings made objectionable. He had piled them sadly away; perhaps she would never come and sit on them again. Perhaps there would never be any more friendly meals together, with what he had brought eking out the straitened household; wine, fruit, truffles when he could find them; she loved truffles. And they had laughed together, and he had written verses to her, and she had called him the Knight of the Doleful Countenance. Was all that done with? If so, he had no reason to live; but it did not mean, he knew, that he would die. He would simply drag on year after year here, a ridiculous, ugly old man, trying to catch a glimpse of her; only that would suffice. But if she did as he had heard she considered doing, and went into a convent — ah, God, that would be the ultimate catastrophe! She would never make a nun. Within days, within a month, she would regret it, and then —

'M. de St Evremond! M. de St Evremond!'

It was Nanon, having hurriedly cast on her hooded cloak; her feet hurried along the uneven pavement; her hands stretched out to him. 'Ah, *monsieur*, I hoped that I would see you, to cheer you! Our little one is dressing tonight to go to Court.'

He felt a great surge of joy pervade him. 'Tonight? Then she is recovered somewhat?'

'Only a little; enough to go out. In fact she could not well refuse His Majesty, who came himself. After he left she bade me comb her hair and cut off the tangles that would not comb, dear me! I will have to dress her hair tonight, for she cannot wear it loose any longer as she used to until the locks grow. And she is going to wear the gown the King gave her in gift. I knew that it would be a joy to you to know. I have seen you pacing the street, my poor *monsieur*, but dared not ask you in. The King — '

'You have had your own troubles, Nanon. Thank God you are faithful to her; why, you have known her far longer than I have, and it seems a part of all my life.'

'We have all had our troubles,' said Nanon

grimly. 'That Madame de Ruz came, weeping and talking of convents, and I was afraid we would be back where he had started; but the Duchess sent her to the rightabout, the good God be thanked. Such people are not a necessity.'

'Thank God indeed,' said St Evremond aloud. He stood looking up at the sky as if God could indeed be seen there. Nanon made her farewells and hastened back to the house in case Hortense needed her. Going up the steps she cast a fleeting glance back at the upright figure of the queer old man, smiling to himself, staring at the sky with the wind stirring his straight grey locks beneath the old-fashioned cap. There was no doubt who was the love of *his* life; and he seemed content if only she were so. He asked nothing more.

39

In the winter of 1684 there was a great frost, so hard that nothing like it had been remembered since before old men were young, when Henry VIII had ridden with his bride Jane Seymour along the ice to the Tower. Now, booths were set up on the frozen river, oxen were roasted there, hot chestnuts sold by vendors, blowing on their fingers to rid them of the icy cold. Society learned to skate and to toboggan; many a fine lady was seen, wrapped in furs and with her hands in a great muff, pushed by admirers smoothly across the ice to the booths, where there was much diversion.

St Evremond planned a picnic for Hortense, to be eaten on the ice. Now that she was meeting the world again he never tired of ways to divert her, remembering Madame de Ruz and the threat of convents; his Duchess must be made to see, once again, that the world was a place to enjoy, not fly from. So they nibbled cooked game and pies and syllabubs and drank wine, all brought wrapped carefully in baskets by the servants; it was even more of a success than a former attempt of St Evremond's had been, for not long ago he had hired a celebrity who played the flute, to entertain Hortense for a whole evening. The picnic did not break up till it grew dark, and torches flared on the thick ice, casting flickering shadows. After that St Evremond had two more reasons to tease Hortense and make her laugh; she had subjugated Sidney Godolphin, the wealthy widower and breeder of racehorses, and M. Bonrepaus himself, who had replaced Barillon, the French envoy.

Nevertheless he was a little troubled about her. She who had always been so sweet-tempered — the sweetest person alive, considering all the trials she had borne — was often ill-humoured nowadays, like a fractious child recovering from an illness. He waited, and found the reason; absinthe. Hortense would take a little nip, and then another; no doubt it was to keep her spirits up when nothing was happening and she had time to remember de Banier. St Evremond redoubled his efforts to entertain her, joke with her, make her laugh; but sometimes she quarrelled with him out of sheer perversity, and then he would be the unhappiest man in London till they made it up again, which they always did.

★ ★ ★

The Court was at Whitehall. In the Long Gallery, a fire had been lit against the February cold, and by the evening the card-players had chilly fingers. The King strolled about amongst them, watching the game; particularly that played by Louise Portsmouth and Hortense Mazarin. The one was as deft a player as he knew, while the other would cheat shamelessly. After the play he sat by the ladies and toyed with his little dogs, who as usual were everywhere, and a page played the lute and sang; Charles' eyes roved through the dimness to appraise each one of his mistresses. One now was no more than a friend; Barbara Cleveland in her day had been a red-gold beauty, savage as a wild cat, greedy and unscrupulous. He had never had any illusions about her, and in the end had let her take other lovers than himself. Her children were dear to him.

Then there was Louise. How matronly she seemed with the new fashion from France, the *fontange*, discreetly arranged on her piled brown curls, one of which was coaxed to fall over her shoulder! Of them all, Fubbs was the one he had loved best; and that in spite of all he knew about her trafficking with French interests, her greed — most women were greedy — her lack of courage during the Popish Plot, when she had had her gear packed ready to return to France. Perhaps it was because she reminded him of his sister Minette — that last farewell of theirs — that he had this fondness. The fairest jewel of all . . . He felt tears spring to his eyes, and hastily looked away; his glance fell on Hortense Mazarin. What a handsome woman, what a beauty! Her hair, which she wore dressed now in the Court fashion, had grown back where it had been cut; but the locks were white. It suited her, brought out the smooth quality of her skin; she had never needed paint. She was as she had used to be, fragrant, elegant, witty, amusing; and yet a certain joy had gone out of her. 'It comes to all of us,' murmured Charles. His thoughts flew to his beloved son Monmouth, whom he had seen secretly not more than days since; the boy had travelled from Holland. They might never meet again; he dared not bring Monmouth home, because of his own brother who must inherit.

It came to him that he was feeling old. He had a sore on his heel that had troubled him for some days; this morning he had had to follow the hunt in a carriage. Thinking of the women he had once loved he knew that he could assess them, now, as friends, no more. There was Nell, there was Moll, there was Catherine. His wife had endured more than most women. There had been difficulties in the past, but now everything was smooth; she had accepted the situation. A wise woman, Catherine; had he been a better man he might have made her the husband she deserved.

The singing stopped, the fire died down; the women's great skirts at last swept curtsying; he looked down with a kind of tenderness on Hortense's whitening hair. Any other woman would have dyed it. But she . . . natural as a nymph, a goddess, he'd called her. He was glad she had come to England.

Later, in his bed, he fell into a fitful sleep. When he awoke it was morning and they were waiting to dress him, shave him. Thank God he had never had to endure the ceremony of Louis at Versailles! He could still put on his own shirt and fasten his own breeches.

The barber came to shave him. Before the man started Charles felt a fit of dizziness overcome him and went into a little closet where he kept drugs to ease it. He had closed the door and those outside waited a long time. When at last they went in, the King was lying in a seizure.

★ ★ ★

Hortense heard of it, and, for the second time recently, prayed. It was not that she need fear continuing under a new King who was Mary of Modena's husband; as the Queen's cousin all doors would be open to her. But she was sad at Charles's passing; it was not so long ago that he had comforted her, and now she could not go and comfort him; he would be surrounded by officials, lackeys, surgeons, relations; all those who waited to see a king die. For if he did not die, what then? Would he be happy as an invalid, dragging out his days, unable even to go down to Windsor to fish in the river as he loved to do, and feed his waterfowl in St James's Park? No, it would be better for him to die. She prayed for a speedy passing for him.

It was not so. He lingered many hours in agony, with the doctors' tormenting recipes of hot irons applied to the head, much bleeding, nauseous draughts. The people waited for news in the streets and London was silent. A whisper went round, arisen from God knew where, perhaps a groom at the Palace who had got it from Chiffinch of the backstairs. *I am sorry to be so unconscionable a time a-dying.* Wry laughter in his mind, watching the solemn, avid faces . . .

But he died. They whispered that Father Huddleston, who had helped the King escape after Worcester in Cromwell's time, had been secretly brought and had given Charles the Last Sacraments after hearing his confession behind a curtain. That was good, she thought; it meant that whatever Charles must still endure he would see the face of God, in the end. 'He was no greater a sinner than I,' she breathed, and wept for him.

★ ★ ★

It might not have been that she herself was a more important personage now that the Queen was her cousin and she had an invitation to the most magnificent coronation yet held in the annals of England; but Marianne de Bouillon invited herself to stay. Marianne had grown stouter with the years, much more the *grande dame* then formerly: she boasted that there was talk of her son's betrothal to the niece of Madame de Maintenon, the grave lady who for some time had ruled the King. Hortense stared; it did not sound like Louis that he should be grave, say his prayers, turn the Court to quiet pursuits, and obey, for that was what it came to, the Church in the personification of a woman who had never been beautiful except for her eyes, seated in a hooded chair away from draughts. 'It is since the poisonings, I think, that the King has changed, although nothing was permitted to be said openly at the time, and Madame de Montespan stayed on in her rooms for two years. But that was the end of her, whatever they say. She had borne the King eight children and is now very stout — ' Marianne looked down with complacence at her own figure — 'and she is not *persona grata* any more than our sister Olympe, who is banished. Oh, if you could see Olympe! She has coarsened, like a great bloated spider weaving its webs to trap flies.'

'I do not want to hear about her,' put in Hortense, fearful that Marianne might mention Olympe's son. She broke in with chatter about the recent coronation, and how beautiful the Queen had looked with all her rich dark hair hanging to her waist beneath the jewelled crown, and even her shoes made of cloth of gold. 'And there was music written especially for it which they say will never be forgotten, though God forbid it may have to be used again too soon.'

'The new King seems in reasonable health, for all his wenching,' said Marianne dryly.

257

★ ★ ★

'Why do you weep for King Charles still? He was no more to you than another lover.' St Evremond's voice was petulant; there had been no jollity today, and he suspected Hortense of drinking absinthe again; certainly Lord Galway had sent her over a crate of the best Irish whiskey.

She was in bed, feeling ill. 'He was much more,' she said. 'He was a comforter and a friend. He gave me money when I had none. Many consider him a wicked man, but I know he was lonely, embittered, even secretive because it must be; separated from those he loved best or robbed of them by death. Death! Why does it not come and take me? I have nothing to live for.'

'You have your friends,' he said gently.

'Friends? They will forget me within a week of my death. I wonder,' she said, turning her head away, 'what they will say of me when I am dead? Perhaps nothing. That would be the worst fate of all.'

St Evremond went away accordingly and composed a charming little epitaph, which made her laugh and receive him in a friendly way again: but most days she was not herself. One day Nanon ran in with the eyes starting out of her head.

'It is the Queen, madame, the Queen! And we have no time to get you dressed.'

'Tell my cousin that I am ill in bed, and bid her come up.' When the quiet, elegant Italian Queen of James II came into the room, she had her apology ready.

'Madame, I cannot curtsy to you. Forgive my state. I have not been well.'

'That is exactly why I came to see you,' said Mary of Modena in Italian. 'I had heard — how one does hear things at St James's! — that you were not as you should be, and I thought that I would call on you. It is a trifle wearisome to be a Queen, Hortense. Everyone curtsies. Your sick-bed is a relief to me, although I grieve to see you ill.'

She had settled herself in a chair, and Hortense noticed that she was much enveloped in scarves and veils. Why? Could she be *enceinte* again? It was some time since she had given birth to her other children, who had all died.

'You have discovered my secret,' said Mary of Modena, watching her. 'Be discreet and do not babble of it; I have had the utmost difficulty in keeping it from my step-daughter, the Princess of Denmark, who would at once have written of it to her elder sister, the Princess of Orange. There is a feeling in the country that when my husband dies, her husband should be King.'

'William of Orange? Why, madame?' Hortense opened her eyes wide. She put out a hand, and murmured congratulations on the coming child. The Queen seemed not to hear her. 'They have tried to pry into my secret,' she said. 'The other day, when I was being dressed, the Princess of Denmark — I can no longer call her Anne — came and tried to see, almost by thrusting herself between my maids, whether I was pregnant or not. I think she went away unsatisfied; but it would all go by dispatch to Holland. You, cousin, are the only person I can trust. I know that you will not let this become common gossip. I should dislike that very much.'

'I hope greatly that all goes well,' said Hortense. 'I myself have borne five children, and know none of them. I hope your child will bring you joy.'

'And joy to the people of England,' said Mary of Modena. 'But . . . they are difficult to understand, these English people. My husband is no better with them than I. He is used to the navy, where a commander issues a command and it is done, so! But it is not like that with these people. My husband has determined that they shall return to the Catholic Faith, and I do not think that they will do it because he asks them.'

'King Charles, whom they loved, died a Catholic.'

'But secretly, or else it could not have been managed. The people have not forgotten Titus Oates, liar as he was, and his Popish Plot, and the poor wretches who were tortured and in the end hanged, although they were innocent.'

'You think . . . there may be trouble if the King tries to have his way?'

'I greatly fear it, although as his wife I may say nothing.' The beautiful face took on animation, and she smiled. 'I had him up before two confessors the other day because of his women, and he has promised to forswear them; and for myself, I went to take the waters at Bath, as a result of which I think this child was conceived healthily in me.'

'I pray that it may continue so,' said Hortense. It was not so. The child was born safely, and was a boy. But the fact of a Catholic heir aroused memories of the Popish Plot, the murder of Sir Edmund Berry Godfrey which had been blamed on the Papists; a hundred things, going back to the Spanish Armada and the reign of Bloody Mary. The King fell foul of six Anglican bishops, whom he placed in the

Tower. Men in England began to talk of a Protestant wind, which would waft William of Orange to their shores. The memory of poor Monmouth, executed for an abortive rebellion in the year of the accession, had grown dim. A tune called 'Lillibulero' began to be whistled and shouted; and all the time the year grew colder, with fogs and damp creeping up from the Thames.

On one such night, the Queen of England, her child in her arms, stole out to hide under the bridges and endure the cold; presently a gascon nobleman, the Comte de Lauzun, who had sworn to bring her safely to France, came and took her away; the hazard of the Channel was crossed; King Louis greeted her at Versailles. Presently the sound of drums were heard through England; the Prince of Orange had landed, and King James put up no fight. He joined his wife in France after being brought back in ignominy, then allowed to escape, for he was of value to few. King William and Queen Mary were monarchs of England, Protestants whom nothing would change.

★ ★ ★

Hortense was afraid. Her cousin's husband had continued her pension from King

Charles; it was too much to hope that William of Orange would do so. Should she go back to France? 'If you do,' said the Seigneur de St Evremond grimly, 'it will mean that you will be made a professed nun.' The lawsuit still went back and forth between herself and Mazarin; in the end, Mazarin won. Hortense moved out of her house in St James's, which she could no longer afford; then, as she could no longer afford Kensington either, to a little house in Chelsea, with a view of the river. Her spirits revived once her goods were brought and arranged in the pretty rooms; she could entertain here, not on so large a scale as formerly, but a little.

Almost the first letter that came was one from Mazarin.

It was typical; she read it over the twisted lips. As the subject of a heretic monarch, her soul would perish from spiritual gangrene. She wrote a short reply, very much to the point. She would come back if he paid her debts.

40

William III was neither vindictive nor lacking in humour, and as soon as much other pressing business was concluded he set about the matter of restoring Hortense's pension. It was time; she was so deeply in debt that she hardly dared go out of the Chelsea house, and Mazarin, in France, had once more appealed to the Council for her extradition and his own claim to all of Cardinal Mazarin's fortune. The Council gave her three months to return to her husband; if she did not do so, the whole of the money was his.

But Hortense had friends, and they saw that she was not arrested, either for the French argument or the English one. Her gambling parties at Chelsea continued with *éclat*. Two eminent philosophers, one French and one Dutch, attended these and were entranced with her; and out of the past, the long, long forgotten past, came a little hook-nosed figure, Jean de la Fontaine. Back at his lodgings, he wrote a poem about her beauty and grace.

. . . ce n'est pas tout;
Les qualités du coeur; ce n'est pas tout
encore.

But although her heart might be in the right place she was still drinking too much absinthe. It had not impaired her beauty yet — it was considered astonishing that her grand-daughter across the Channel, Mademoiselle de Bellefonds, should be growing up in the mould of her grandmother and that there was little to choose between the appearance of the ageing woman and the young girl — but it had worked havoc with her temper. Poor old St Evremond bore the brunt of it, never mentioning to anyone that she owed him seven hundred pounds. At Lord Rochester's supper and ball Hortense danced till dawn; at another party, she brought forty dozen fireworks to enliven the night.

St Evremond called one day; it was not about the money. He wanted to tell Hortense of news that had just come for him; permission, if he wished, after all these years, to return to France, which he had been forced to leave after mocking the Peace of the Pyrenees — *mon Dieu,* that had been in the year of King Louis' marriage! An exile ever since, he felt as all Frenchmen feel about their native land; it is like no other. But he could not bring himself to abandon Hortense. He would tell her of it; perhaps it would please her. Lately she had been praying in her chapel a great deal; he hoped it did not mean that she was thinking of convents again.

She was there when he was admitted to the house, and as an old friend he went straight in to the chapel. Hortense knelt on the floor, her arms about Father Milon's neck. The shock sent the blood back to St Evremond's heart. Did she, then, whore with her priest? Alas!

Some sound he made caused her to turn her head, and at the look on his face she burst out laughing. 'My friend, I am fitting him with earrings,' she said. 'I have just pierced his ears.'

'It is very painful,' said Father Milon solemnly. His ears bled a little. 'Wipe them with a linen rag and it will soon stop,' said Hortense heartlessly. 'But we must put these in now, and you must wear them while the ears are healing. Otherwise the hole will simply close up again.'

But she was not, at heart, gay then. She had just had word from France, not akin to St Evremond's. 'They say vile things of me!' she told him. 'I will write — how I will write — answering each *écrit défammatoire*. I have as much to say as they, as many wrongs as he had!' And she sat down at her writing-table and scrawled a long letter, while St Evremond watched hopelessly. At the end she brought it to him to read. 'Too long, too passionate,' he told her. 'Let me shorten it a little, alter the phrases which will do you harm.'

'No.' She stamped her foot. 'You know very well that a wife ought not to leave her husband; if I did so it was because he was bad, very bad. And as for his lawyer, damn him; he has neither truth, judgment nor decency.'

But St Evremond kept returning patiently to the charge, and in the end she threw the letter at him and let him change it.

Next day he came to her. 'It may not be necessary to send our letter,' he said. 'Opinion is changing in France. They say Mazarin is a madman and dresses like one, or like a beggar. Piety runs riot in his brain as though there were a worm there. 'His wife is exempted from ordinary rules,' they say when they see him. 'One recognises that she is justified.' '

He saw her go over and fill two glasses with absinthe and bring him one, draining her own. He shook his head and she drank his glass also. 'They have taken their time, have they not?' she burst out in fury. 'When I think of what ought to be mine — great jewels whose appearance I have forgotten, and which are finer than any at this Court; palaces in Paris and houses in the country, with estates and farms which would bring me rent-money which has gone all these years to *him*! Can you wonder that I complain? Only an angel would keep silent.'

'You are an angel,' said the old man loyally. But to a friend he wrote, 'God give me patience! But she does not disturb a man of my age.' He would surely be dead before her; while they both lived, he would enjoy her company.

Fewer did so than formerly. As well as the rumours of her debts, the stories of her drinking had got about; Lord Galway's presents of Irish whiskey were noted, and other things. When one went to dine with Duchess Mazarin these days, it was almost *de rigueur* to leave a sum of money under the plate afterwards, as if it had been an eating-house. Many of her invitations were simply ignored; often she and St Evremond sat down to a grandly laden table, nothing of which had been paid for, with no guests.

But there was St Evremond, and there was Mustapha, who had always adored her;

Nanon had gone. One day a pleasant thing happened; she had been winning at the tables lately, and instead of spending the sum recklessly, she was able to hoard it. When St Evremond next came, she placed in his hands the debt she owed him. She was smiling and gay.

'I will only take it in order that I may help you,' he said. And he did, as he always had; little presents, food and wine and butter and game-pie, were brought each day; she did not starve. Looking at her one day he saw that her hair was quite grey. Why had he not noticed it before? The answer was in his own mind, clearly; to him she would always be the beautiful Duchess, whom he had first seen almost a quarter of a century ago.

* * *

It was June. She was standing by her window with the curtains drawn and the casements open, looking out on the river with its little boats; the great barges did not come by often. Suddenly she dropped to the floor and remained lying there, breathing heavily; she was found by Mustapha when he came in. 'Madame, madame!' he cried, then when there was no answer ran, with the tears streaming down his face, for help;

he and the under-valet got her to bed. They sent for St Evremond, who sat by her bedside faithfully. The doctors came and did what they always did in such cases and most others; they bled her, without result. St Evremond watched the knife cut into the white arm with almost physical pain. Through his tears, he went to the table and wrote to her family, in France. A fortnight passed without any change in her condition; when at last her eyes opened they looked large in the pale face.

'You are here . . . my Knight . . . what has happened?' She did not seem to know that she had been ill, or remember anything that had occurred. She reached out a weak hand to him; he took it and kissed it.

'Shall I send for a priest?' he whispered to her. Father Milon did not live in the house.

'No,' she whispered, 'no priests.' Her eyes closed again, and she slept.

Presently she wakened to be told that the doctors had come again. 'I will not have them,' she said, 'send them away. Stay with me. I need no one but you.'

A few days later she had a further attack. St Evremond took brandy and poured it down her throat; she swallowed it, but did not know him. Then, of his own volition, he sent for Father Milon; she must not die without the sacraments. He went out while the priest did what had to be done; afterwards, he went back to Hortense, lying supine with Christ on her tongue. She seemed to be growing weaker. The days passed, and the nights. Suddenly, one morning, with the early summer sun shining in at the window, St Evremond knew that she was about to die. He knelt by her; he saw her face grow suddenly translucent, beautiful, more so than it had ever been. Then she died. It was eight o'clock. His tears fell on her still hands.

★ ★ ★

Marianne de Bouillon and Hortense's son Paul-Jules, the one she had borne after being stuck in the chimney, had arrived off the packet at Dover. They stopped at an inn for food, and while there saw a gazette; in it there was news of Hortense. The Duchess Mazarin would not live for more than a few hours.

'We will get nothing but debts, dogs, birds and a negro slave,' said Marianne, whose grandeur did not rule out a certain practicality. Paul-Jules said nothing. He did not remember his mother, but there was no point in seeing her when she was dead.

271

They stepped on the boat again before it turned round, and went back to France.

* * *

St Evremond had one more duty to perform. In mid-August, with poor Mustapha and Hortense's executors, they shipped the coffin on board a packet and travelled with it across the Channel to Normandy. In the church a distraught, odd man waited; it was Mazarin. By law they must leave the body with him.

* * *

He would not bury her. She could not escape him now; from time to time he would lay his hand on the coffin, as if again to possess the body that lay within. He travelled with her to his Breton estate, where once she had been happy visiting his father; he took her then to Vincennes, to Bourbon, to Alsace, along the same road they had travelled together when she was heavy with child. The journeys went on for months and grew to be a legend; simple folk brought their rosaries to lay on the coffin, or their sick children to touch it. The Duchess Mazarin had been a saint, they began to say.

At last they stopped at a Norman convent.

The Abbess, a gentle woman, came to the distraught Mazarin. 'She is dead, my son,' she said. 'The dead should be left in peace.'

'She gave me no peace — all my life, since I was a young man and saw her at ten years old — '

'It is the part of a Christian to forgive. You yourself will find peace when you have done so. Let her rest here, beside the tomb where her uncle the Cardinal lies. Her soul is elsewhere, not in the coffin. Let her rest.'

He laid his head in his hands suddenly. What had it all been for, his whole life's journeying? Perhaps soon he could rest also, as the nun said. If he had known, he had twenty more years to live; but he did not know, and went away, leaving the body of Hortense beside the body of the long-dead Cardinal. There they would lie, everyone thought, in peace.

★ ★ ★

It was not to be. Almost a century later the Revolution broke out and the bones of the great, kings, cardinals and princes, were dragged from their tombs, insulted, and thrown away. A mob came to the Norman abbey and dragged out the bones of Mazarin and Hortense. There was no jewellery to take, and the bones stank. They put them on a bonfire they had made, and kicked the ashes.

THE END

THE GREENWAY
Jane Adams

When Cassie and her twelve-year-old cousin Suzie had taken a short cut through an ancient Norfolk pathway, Suzie had simply vanished ... Twenty years on, Cassie is still tormented by nightmares. She returns to Norfolk, determined to solve the mystery.

FORTY YEARS
ON THE WILD FRONTIER
Carl Breihan & W. Montgomery

Noted Western historian Carl Breihan has culled from the handwritten diaries of John Montgomery, grandfather of co-author Wayne Montgomery, new facts about Wyatt Earp, Doc Holliday, Bat Masterson and other famous and infamous men and women who gained notoriety when the Western Frontier was opened up.

TAKE NOW, PAY LATER
Joanna Dessau

This fiction based on fact is the love-turning-to-hate story of Robert Carr, Earl of Somerset, and his wife, Frances.

McLEAN AT THE GOLDEN OWL
George Goodchild
Inspector McLean has resigned from Scotland Yard's CID and has opened an office in Wimpole Street. With the help of his able assistant, Tiny, he solves many crimes, including those of kidnapping, murder and poisoning.

KATE WEATHERBY
Anne Goring
Derbyshire, 1849: The Hunter family are the arrogant, powerful masters of Clough Grange. Their feuds are sparked by a generation of guilt, despair and ill-fortune. But their passions are awakened by the arrival of nineteen-year-old Kate Weatherby.

A VENETIAN RECKONING
Donna Leon
When the body of a prominent international lawyer is found in the carriage of an intercity train, Commissario Guido Brunetti begins to dig deeper into the secret lives of the once great and good.

A TASTE FOR DEATH
Peter O'Donnell

Modesty Blaise and Willie Garvin take on impossible odds in the shape of Simon Delicata, the man with a taste for death, and Swordmaster, Wenczel, in a terrifying duel. Finally, in the Sahara desert, the intrepid pair must summon every killing skill to survive.

SEVEN DAYS FROM MIDNIGHT
Rona Randall

In the Comet Theatre, London, seven people have good reason for wanting beautiful Maxine Culver out of the way. Each one has reason to fear her blackmail. But whose shadow is it that lurks in the wings, waiting to silence her once and for all?

QUEEN OF THE ELEPHANTS
Mark Shand

Mark Shand knows about the ways of elephants, but he is no match for the tiny Parbati Barua, the daughter of India's greatest expert on the Asian elephant, the late Prince of Gauripur, who taught her everything. Shand sought out Parbati to take part in a film about the plight of the wild herds today in north-east India.

THE DARKENING LEAF
Caroline Stickland

On storm-tossed Chesil Bank in 1847, the young lovers, Philobeth and Frederick, prevent wreckers mutilating the apparent corpse of a young woman. Discovering she is still alive, Frederick takes her to his grandmother's home. But the rescue is to have violent and far-reaching effects . . .

A WOMAN'S TOUCH
Emma Stirling

When Fenn went to stay on her uncle's farm in Africa, the lovely Helena Starr seemed to resent her — especially when Dr Jason Kemp agreed to Fenn helping in his bush hospital. Though it seemed Jason saw Fenn as little more than a child, her feelings for him were those of a woman.

A DEAD GIVEAWAY
Various Authors

This book offers the perfect opportunity to sample the skills of five of the finest writers of crime fiction — Clare Curzon, Gillian Linscott, Peter Lovesey, Dorothy Simpson and Margaret Yorke.

DOUBLE INDEMNITY
— MURDER FOR INSURANCE
Jad Adams

This is a collection of true cases of murderers who insured their victims then killed them — or attempted to. Each tense, compelling account tells a story of cold-blooded plotting and elaborate deception.

THE PEARLS OF COROMANDEL
By Keron Bhattacharya

John Sugden, an ambitious young Oxford graduate, joins the Indian Civil Service in the early 1920s and goes to uphold the British Raj. But he falls in love with a young Hindu girl and finds his loyalties tragically divided.

WHITE HARVEST
Louis Charbonneau

Kathy McNeely, a marine biologist, sets out for Alaska to carry out important research. But when she stumbles upon an illegal ivory poaching operation that is threatening the world's walrus population, she soon realises that she will have to survive more than the harsh elements . . .

TO THE GARDEN ALONE
Eve Ebbett

Widow Frances Morley's short, happy marriage was childless, and in a succession of borders she attempts to build a substitute relationship for the husband and family she does not have. Over all hovers the shadow of the man who terrorized her childhood.

CONTRASTS
Rowan Edwards

Julia had her life beautifully planned — she was building a thriving pottery business as well as sharing her home with her friend Pippa, and having fun owning a goat. But the goat's problems brought the new local vet, Sebastian Trent, into their lives.

MY OLD MAN AND THE SEA
David and Daniel Hays

Some fathers and sons go fishing together. David and Daniel Hays decided to sail a tiny boat seventeen thousand miles to the bottom of the world and back. Together, they weave a story of travel, adventure, and difficult, sometimes terrifying, sailing.